CW01261491

BRUTAL REVENGE

A THRILLER

BY JAMES RAVEN

,

Published through

Global House Publishing

,

James Raven is a journalist and former television executive

For my grandchildren

'

By the same author

Rollover

Urban Myth

Stark Warning

Arctic Blood

After the Execution

Red Blitz

http://www.james-raven.com/

ONE

The urge to satisfy his own curiosity was really what made Parker come to Glasgow.

It certainly wasn't because he needed the money, not with the bundle from that last blag still gathering dust in a safety deposit box in London. No, it was simply that he wanted to know what that old rascal Andrew Maclean was up to.

It had been three years since they had last worked together, and Maclean's email, which had arrived two days ago, had come out of the blue. Being brief and to the point it had left a thousand questions unanswered.

"If you're still in business Parker, get in touch. I've something wild in mind and I'm pretty sure you'll want in. Andrew."

So Parker had responded, regardless of the fact that he'd been planning to spend a few weeks at the apartment in Marbella before embarking on another caper.

On the phone Maclean had refused to be drawn on the details of what was going down. He'd said only that it would be worth Parker's while to make the journey north.

"Trust me, Phil," he'd said. "You won't be disappointed."

Only now, standing in a shop doorway opposite the entrance to that dingy hotel, did Parker begin to question the wisdom of his decision. Three years is a long time and men change. Perhaps Maclean had changed. Perhaps he was no longer the impetuous young Scotsman whom Parker remembered as being sufficiently blessed with an abundance of both common sense and unquestioning nerve – truly a rare combination of qualities in a man whose chosen profession had been crime.

Perhaps now Maclean was nothing like the man Parker had come to admire during their brief acquaintance, when they had been part of a team that had held up three security vans in London during a single summer.

These days Maclean ran an antiques business, but Parker had heard that he was still a pretty active villain. Maybe he was having a rough time of it and had come up with some hair-brained scheme to make some serious dosh. Times were tough, after all, and it was becoming harder to steal money without taking huge risks. At thirty six Parker wasn't keen to take too many chances for fear of ending up inside again. Life was too short to piss it away in some dingy cell.

It began to rain, and whatever traces of ageing dignity the street had possessed were washed away with the slime. All that was left was a drab collection of dilapidated buildings, shabbily plastered with corrugated iron sheets and large wooden boards that should have displayed For Sale signs, but now issued crude threats in shiny black paint to any young thug from another district who dared to venture beyond them.

What a shithole, Parker thought. Worse than the ugliest manors in London. Both cities had been

,

hammered by the recession, but by the look of it Glasgow would take much longer to recover.

The hotel was one of only three buildings in the whole street that seemed to be occupied, and light from the entrance and ground floor windows fell as carpets across the pavements.

No light was offered by the innumerable street lamps. At some time in the past these had been rendered impotent by a proficient sniper whose grudge against light bulbs must have been pathological in its intensity.

It was because everything here was so decrepit – like a war-torn ghetto – that Parker had begun to have second thoughts. Maybe he was wrong to satisfy curiosity merely for the sake of it. Maybe Maclean had been talking out of his arse when he'd told him it would be worth his while to come here.

Parker took a long, resigned breath and shook his head. Frankly there was no point turning back now. He might as well have the meet and sus it out. If he didn't like the set-up he'd just walk out and get a train back to London. It was as simple as that.

He looked again at the hotel, an unprepossessing place that seemed to be still standing solely by virtue of the fact that it was sandwiched between two other buildings. Had it been detached at birth, Parker felt sure it would have crumbled to the ground long before now. Far beyond it, where the cloud cover ended over the Clyde, the high concrete peaks of the city merged with the molten colour of the evening sky.

He pulled the collar of his raincoat up around his neck and hurried towards the hotel entrance. He chose an inopportune moment to do so, for just then the clouds decided to spend their lot all at once and it came down in a torrent that formed instant puddles in the road.

He was drenched when he went into the hotel and it took only a moment for him to form a puddle of his own on the linoleum floor of the small, grubby reception area.

The proprietor, a big man of about forty-five with a square face and an unsightly five o'clock shadow, was reading a newspaper behind the desk.

He looked up, regarded Parker for a moment, and said, “You must be Parker.”

“How’d you know?”

The guy shrugged. “Because I’m not expecting anyone else and believe it or not we don’t attract much passing trade.”

“You surprise me,” Parker said.

The man cleared his throat. “Mac's expecting you. He’s upstairs. If you'll just wait a minute I'll call him up on the house phone and tell him you're here.”

Parker glanced around the reception area, which didn't say much for the owner's concept of decent living. The range of types to be impressed by the peeling wallpaper, the rickety stairs and the musty smell, would be limited indeed. Whores and their horny customers probably formed the bulk of the business.

“He's on his way down,” the proprietor said, replacing the phone and returning to his paper without another word.

,

Barely a minute later Parker heard the familiar high-pitched voice behind him and, turning, saw Maclean at the bottom of the stairs, grinning.

"Well, well," he beamed at Parker. "Long time no see."

Parker noticed immediately that three years had done little to change the man. At least on the outside he was the Andrew Maclean Parker remembered. He was about thirty and looked lean and fit. He retained the confident swagger that Parker remembered so well. There was also the air of insolence and the familiar look of perpetual amusement on his thin, ruddy face. He stood roughly six feet tall – the same height as Parker - and was wearing a cardigan over polo sweater and jeans.

He shoved out a hand. "Good to see you, Phil. I've been looking forward to working with you again. What is it now? Three years."

Parker returned the greeting, adding, "Don't jump the gun, Andy. I'm here to see what it's all about. That's all."

The ever-present grin widened into an elaborate smile that conjured up a network of laughter lines around the eyes and mouth. It occurred to Parker that this precarious profession of theirs rarely allowed a person's sense of humour to be preserved in such a fine old state of health.

"Course," Maclean said. "Didn't think otherwise. But as I said on the phone, I guarantee that you'll be interested."

"Well I fucking hope so. It's a long way to come just for a chat."

,

Maclean dropped his voice. “Any problems getting away at such short notice?”

Parker shook his head. “I’ve got nothing on the go right now. In fact I was on the verge of buggering off to Spain when you got in touch.”

“What about the wife? She can’t have been too happy?”

“We got divorced a year ago,” Parker said. “I live alone.”

“Sorry to hear that.”

“Don’t be. It’d been a long time coming. We pissed each other off big time and the last straw came when I found out she was shagging someone at work.”

“Ouch! That must have been painful.”

“Yeah, it was, but it didn’t take me long to get over it after she left.”

“Did she move in with the other bloke?”

“No way. He’s married with kids. She went back to live with her mum in Brighton.”

“Life sucks,” Maclean said.

Parker shrugged. “Enough of the small talk. Anyone else involved in this caper?”

Maclean nodded. “Two more bodies. You might even know them.”

“Where are they?”

“Upstairs.”

Maclean turned to the guy behind the desk who was still absorbed in his newspaper. “Make sure we're not disturbed for the next couple of hours, Donald,” he said.

TWO

Maclean led the way to a first floor room. It was pretty small and contained a round table and a lumpy leather sofa.

A bare light bulb hung from the ceiling and emitted a dull orange glow.

"We use this place for poker sessions," Maclean said. "But everyone's skint so there's no action this week."

There were two men sitting at the table. One of them Parker recognised instantly as Pat Hodge. They had never met but he had been pointed out to Parker at a party once.

Rumour had it the guy was a genuine grade-A psycho, and Parker could see why such speculation was rife.

There was that calm, unnerving expression and those wide staring eyes that belied his boyish looks and made one wonder if it was not the devil himself looking out from behind a mask. He had the kind of deadpan face that deters women from parking themselves in the same railway carriage.

His reputation was not unknown to Parker. Hodge once shot dead a security guard during a wages snatch in Birmingham, an achievement that had earned him the nickname The Cowboy. He was never charged with the murder even though the cops were convinced he was responsible. His alibis were watertight and there were no witnesses to finger him. It was common knowledge in the trade that he did it. But knowing it and proving it are two very different things.

Maclean introduced Parker to Hodge first and Parker was thankful that the latter did not feel obliged to get up and shake his hand.

Hodge simply looked up from the table, nodded almost imperceptibly, and said, “I've heard a lot about you, Parker.”

“I've heard a lot about you, too,” Parker said.

Hodge tried his hand at smiling, but the effort behind this gesture was fairly evident.

“Whatever you've heard it's all lies,” he said. “I'm really a little angel at heart.”

“I’m sure you are.”

Hodge was a Scouser and Parker judged him to be in his early thirties. He was tall and athletically built with a shock of black wavy hair. There was a two-inch scar beneath his right eye and one high up on his forehead.

In a way he reminded Parker of himself as he was some years ago. He too had shouldered a reputation for being a hard bastard, and with each new acquaintance he struck he had sensed the other man's cold, almost scornful appraisal of him.

It was the reason he had got involved in so many scraps. There was always some young head case on the scene who wanted to prove that he was harder and tougher. Luckily for Parker his scars weren’t visible until he bared his torso, which was why he rarely did it in public, even around the swimming pool in Spain. The damage to his stomach and chest caused by two knife attacks was not a pleasant sight.

,

The other character, who Parker didn't know, got up from his chair. He was short compared with the rest of them — not more than five foot six — with a pale, aquiline face. The beak-shaped nose was inordinately large and looked as though it had been stuck on as an after-thought.

He was dressed in an off-the-peg suit from one of the big chain stores, but the jacket hung well enough and went a long way towards hiding up an incipient beer gut. He was almost bald and there were deep trenches around the mouth and eyes that would have made it impossible for him to get away with any white lies about being under fifty.

His smile was bright and engaging and his dentures a tribute to whoever had made them.

Maclean introduced them. "Robert Stewart, meet Phil Parker. An old friend."

Stewart extended a hand towards Parker. "Hello Parker," he said. "I can see you don't remember me."

"Should I?"

"Eight years ago. Strangeways. I was doing a stretch for burglary and you did a stretch before they shifted you out to an open prison. We mixed with the same crowd for a bit."

Parker nodded as if in recognition, though the truth was he could barely remember who his various cell-mates had been on that, his one and only spell inside.

"From Glasgow are you?" Parker asked because he couldn't think of anything else to say.

Stewart grimaced. "Now I ask you, do I really look like one of those scruffy graduates from the gangs?"

Parker had to admit that he did not.

"I was born and bred in Edinburgh," Stewart said with an exaggerated roll of the `r's. "Purest and finest town in all of Scotland without a doubt."

"So I've heard," Parker said. "I've never been there myself."

"Make it your dying wish then. If the castle is the last thing you ever see you'll die a happy man and no mistake."

Parker liked Stewart. The guy gave off a good vibe and he thought they could probably get on. And to Parker first impressions counted for a lot. He had always trusted his initial instincts and they had rarely let him down.

Anxious to get down to business, Maclean said, "Come on lads. Let's be seated. We've a lot to get through."

Parker hung up his raincoat and took off his jacket. He ran a hand through his thick fair hair and rainwater sprinkled his face. It was warm in the room, and stuffy. A thick cloud of cigarette smoke floated above the table like a shapeless ghost attracted to the light.

Maclean went into another room and returned a moment later carrying a tray on which he'd placed four cans of Carlsberg lager and four empty glasses.

"Ice cold," he announced. "And there's plenty more where it came from."

When they were all seated around the table, shoulders hunched forward, cigarettes lit, they gave the impression of a late night card school. Maclean handed round the drinks and each glass was filled with alacrity.

Maclean said, "Before we start Phil, how are you fixed for accommodation?"

"I only just arrived," Parker said, "but if I don't want in I'll shove off back to London. If I do I'll try to get a room somewhere for tonight."

"Forget about a room. You can kip at my place. It's not far from here. I've got a spare bedroom."

"Thanks," Parker said. "You sure it won't be a problem?"

"Absolutely not. I live alone too. No one giving me grief. For the time being at least."

Maclean cleared his throat and looked at Parker. "The others know the set-up already and they want in," he said.

Parker nodded. "Will it be just the four of us?"

"As far as I'm concerned four's the absolute minimum needed to pull it off," Maclean said. "I've chosen you lot because I've worked with you before and I know you're good at what you do. I also know I can trust you."

Parker nodded. "Fair enough. So what is it we'd be up against? Bank, security van, factory..."

"It's an island," Maclean said, and Parker stared at him like he'd just grown another head.

Stewart guffawed. "That was my reaction too when he told me," he said. "I thought he must be fucking bonkers."

Maclean went on as if he hadn't been interrupted. "The island's called Stack," he said. "It's in the Hebrides, about forty five miles out from Oban and ten miles off the coast of Mull. Population about two hundred and twenty."

Parker was aghast. "The Hebrides! There's piss all up there but a load of half civilized crofters and bloated sheep."

"Do you mind?" Maclean said. "I'm from the island myself, left when I was a wee lad. Would you say I was only half civilized?" He quickly held up both hands. "No, don't answer that one. I'd rather not know."

Inevitably Stewart laughed and Hodge gave a little chuckle.

"But seriously, Phil," Maclean went on. "You can take my word for it that the Hebrideans are not all gormless crofters. Far from it. You'll see what I mean when you hear what I have to say."

Parker looked at his watch. "You've got a lot of convincing to do, Andy. These days I'm choosy about what I take on. It's an age thing I guess."

"Then I'll give you the best bit first."

"Which is?"

"Gold – and lots of it," Maclean said slowly. "I'm talking millions."

Parker stared at Maclean for a long time, letting the other's words sink in. At length, he said, "I don't get it. How did a fortune in gold find its way onto a fucking island that few people have even heard of?"

Maclean smiled. "It's lost treasure from a sunken wreck. A Spanish galleon to be exact. The ship sank off the coast of Stack about four hundred years ago."

"You have got to be shittin' me," Parker said.

,

Maclean shook his head. “I’m deadly serious. And let me tell you it’s fucking amazing. I didn’t believe it either until I saw it with my own eyes.”

Parker arched his brow. “I thought treasure went out with Long John Silver.”

“Trust me it's up there on that little island just waiting to be grabbed,” Maclean said. “All we have to do is go and help ourselves to it. I’ve already got a few dealers lined up to take it off our hands. They’ll pay top dollar.”

Parker sat back in his chair. His mouth had gone dry, as though it had been sprayed with powder. He knew that if they told him the whole score now he'd be to some extent committed, at least in their eyes, and he wanted to avoid that. But at the same time his curiosity had been aroused. He wanted to know precisely what Maclean had up his sleeve and why he was so sure of himself.

“All right,” Parker said, coming to a decision, “So I'll take your word for it that there's treasure up there. Now you can tell me who it belongs to, how that person came by it, and how the fuck you intend to swipe it.”

THREE

In theory the treasure belonged to the Crown, but it was unlikely that the Receiver of Wrecks would ever know that it had been discovered three months earlier, quite by chance, in just forty feet of water less than five hundred yards off the island of Stack.

The story of a sunken Spanish treasure ship somewhere beneath the waters of the Inner Hebrides had been passed down through the ages. Historians believed it was part of the Spanish Armada and that it went down in a violent storm off the Isle of Mull in 1588.

Ancient records showed that some Armada galleons headed round the north of Scotland to escape the English and at least one of them was laden with gold and jewellery.

Over the years scores of professional treasure hunters and salvage teams had gone in search of the mystery wreck. But, as it turned out, they had been looking in the wrong places. No one had ever explored the possibility that the ship had met ill-fortune close to the sheer south-facing cliffs of Stack.

Yet it was there, over four hundred years later, that one Ruari MacDonald, aged eighteen, had come across it.

That day was warm and sunny. The wind that usually belts down from the Minch was having a rest and the isles of the Inner Hebrides were at peace with the elements.

,

Young Ruari, anxious to make use of his recently acquired aqualung, had managed to persuade his father to take him out to the string of half-submerged rocks below the island's high basaltic cliffs.

He'd chosen that particular spot because he'd never before explored it. Unknowingly, he had swum above the wreck for several minutes on that day before his attention was drawn to an alien shape that stood out in the swirling grey water. He was compelled by curiosity to take a closer look. He propelled himself downwards and the sea floor rose to meet him, a rolling, twisting terrain of various colours over which scores of tiny fish hovered with lethargic grace. When he reached the dark oblong shape that protruded above the sea floor, he found it had been uncovered by a subsidence in the floor at that point. It was encrusted in a mass of thick black scabs that in turn were partially covered by hard green coral growth.

He drew a long sharp knife from his belt and worked at the scabs of black until he had chipped away about five square inches of it. He hit metal then and moved his efforts to another part of the object.

It took only a little while for him to realize it was a cannon. There aren't many things that resemble it in shape and size.

Feverishly he swam over the cannon, running his fingers delicately along its rough top, and then began to slice away indiscriminately with his knife at other bits of coral growth and black encrustations that did not seem to merge perfectly with the scene as a whole.

It took him only thirty more seconds to stumble on the wreck. Very little remained of the huge, once proud vessel because over the years it had broken down into heaps of decomposed wood and rusty metal.

Some of it, thankfully, was in the grip of that ubiquitous black substance which looked for all the world as if it had been poured over parts of the wreck while molten hot and then allowed to solidify.

Ruari explored the area while keeping a careful eye on his watch. In his mind he was already making plans for coming back another time, equipped then with a full tank of air and a pick.

Finally it was time to surface. He had almost used up the air in his tank and probably had just enough to get back up.

He decided to take a piece of the wreck with him as proof of his discovery. He lowered himself to his knees, cut away a chunk of the black substance which enveloped a likely part of the wreck, and then gouged out a fragment of what appeared to be more coral growth from underneath. It felt like wood, he thought, and there were several sharp bits sticking out from it.

It was a lump about the size of an orange and he was able to hold it in one hand as he struck out towards the surface.

When just that one piece of coral was later broken up it was found to contain seven gold coins.

,

*

Naturally Ruari MacDonald's discovery caused a lot of excitement on the island. In the week that followed Ruari went down time and again to the wreck and brought up gold coins and small artefacts by the handful.

Others who knew how to dive took turns as well and among the items they brought to the surface was a silver dinner plate, more gold and silver coins, a few pewter spoons, gold rings, and ornate necklaces and brooches.

Most of the objects had been remarkably well preserved under that strange black concretion which had prevented them from being attacked by corrosive elements over the centuries.

Since it was such a close-knit community there was no question of finders-keepers. It was assumed right from the start that although Ruari had found the wreck and its treasure, it belonged to them all.

Meanwhile Ruari and the other divers plundered the wreck without thought to its archaeological value.

And after two weeks they'd collected all the treasure they could find. They had unearthed more than fifteen thousand coins, most of them gold, plus a sizeable collection of small and obviously valuable artefacts.

Most of the islanders, particularly the older ones, looked on the treasure a gift from God. For so long they had faced hard times. The dwindling population of 220, which had once numbered 1,500, was rapidly approaching danger level and it was feared by all that Stack would join the list of Hebridean islands that had become uninhabited owing to the decline in their populations.

On top of this there was no longer a fishing industry on the island where once it had thrived, and the islanders were these days just managing to make ends meet through some tourism and by earning a few extra pounds from side-line occupations such as weaving and oyster catching.

There were other islands in both the inner and outer Hebrides in the same sorrowful situation as Stack. Each in itself a tragedy of modern times, suffering now because they had long ago been left behind by the inexorable march of progress.

But Stack differed now from those other islands in one significant respect. It had not been forsaken by God. He had blessed the island with a great and wonderful gift, a gift that was surely meant to be used to secure a future for its inhabitants. This was something many of the islanders came firmly to believe. And it was this belief which led eventually to the momentous decision that was taken.

FOUR

The meeting was called on a Saturday night and all the islanders, except the children and a few old folk who were housebound, went along. It took place in the church hall, which was really nothing more than a huge corrugated iron shed with backless wooden benches inside and a sad-looking excuse for a pulpit.

There was a hushed, almost reverent silence, when Alastair MacDonald, Ruari's father, stood up. He was one of six of the island's most respected family heads who were sitting on the bench at the front of the hall behind the pulpit.

He removed his fraying cloth cap and coughed to clear his throat.

Having got the attention of all those present, he stepped forward and stood next to the pulpit, a stout red-cheeked man with short clipped hair.

He welcomed everyone by saying, “I've no need to tell you why you're here. You all know well enough what we've got to be discussing tonight. I intend to start things rolling myself by stating that I, as father of the lad who found the actual wreck, fully support the view held by Ross Mor.” He turned and gestured with his hand towards the man who was sitting on one end of the bench behind him. “I know many more of you do as well, but there might be some among you who do not agree. Well, you can put your views to him in just a minute.

“But first of all I would like to thank God

publicly here tonight for what he has sent us. With the money we are sure to be getting for the treasure we need not worry about our financial well-being for years to come. Aye, it is a blessed thought."

Everyone in the hall agreed with him and there was a lot of smiling and nodding of heads before he raised his hands and they became silent.

"But it must be remembered that this wealth is for the island," he went on. "To be used for the good of all of us. Old and young alike will benefit if we are able to use this money wisely to bring prosperity to the island once again."

MacDonald returned to his place on the bench and Ross Mor came forward. Mor was in his late fifties and was one of a family line that stretched way back to before the island's earliest records were kept. He was a big man, well over six feet, with powerful shoulders and an ape-like stance that was curiously threatening. An enormous dark bushy beard completely covered his mouth when it wasn't open and he had brows to match that were like thick fluffy shades over his narrow eyes. His weather-beaten skin was also dark, besides being heavily lined, and this was because at one time the Celtic blood of his family had been mixed with the Nordic.

He hadn't yet recovered from his wife's death five months earlier and so was still a pitiful sight, somber and haggard, his eyes devoid of life and heavily bloodshot.

There was only one bright spot now - Anna, his daughter. But she was twenty already, ripe to become a bride, and he knew that sooner or later she too would have to desert him.

Anna had been very much on his mind when the idea concerning the treasure had come to him. He was in MacDonald's boat at the time, pulling up the rope which Ruari had tied to a sack-full of coins. Perhaps if he hadn't been thinking about his daughter he would have dismissed the crazy notion out of hand; cursed himself for having contemplated such an outrageous stunt.

But the fact was he *had* been thinking about her, wondering how he could possibly make life less of a struggle for her than it had been for her mother.

Anna was sitting in the second row from the front wearing the long summer dress her mother had made for her. She was not a pretty girl by any means. Her nose was too long and her mouth too small; it was clear there was more of her father in her than her mother.

But her body compensated for her less-than-perfect looks. She had large round breasts and small firm buttocks and therefore attracted the attention of the few red-blooded males around her age on the island.

Mor smiled at her and when she smiled back his confidence grew. He turned to his audience and said, “I'm thankful you are all prepared to listen to me. Most of you already know what I'm going to say and I hope you've given it some thought already.”

A woman shouted, “Is it true that you want us to keep the treasure a secret and no report it to the Receiver?”

He grinned. There were no secrets on Stack.

News always spread like wildfire.

"Aye, that's true," he said.

"But would that no be illegal?"

"Aye, it would," he replied. "But as I see it we've got to look out for ourselves if we don't want to be evacuated to the mainland in years to come. The government will not help us, as we all know from bitter experience. So it's up to us, all of us here tonight, to see that there is a future for our young ones here on Stack."

"What exactly are you getting at Ross?" This time it was Angus Campbell, a rugged looking crofter in the front row who was sandwiched between his two heavyweight sons.

"What I'm getting at is this," Mor said. "If we tell the Receiver of God's precious gift to us it'll become the property of the Crown and to be sure we'll be lucky to get a fraction of its worth as our reward for finding it. Plus, it could take years for all the legal matters to be settled. But if we tell no one and then sell the gold ourselves we'll all be wealthy. And we'll all have a future."

A voice from the back said, "But how would we go about it? We can't just put it on eBay."

The remark sparked a nervous burst of laughter which seemed to ease the tension somewhat.

"We'll sell it gradually," Mor said, after a few seconds. "Over a period of many months – to dealers and collectors. We'll make sure that nobody will ever know where it came from."

Mor gave them time to talk it over amongst themselves and more people plucked up the courage to lob questions at him. After a time it became clear

,

that the majority were rather struck on the idea of deceiving the establishment and were merely seeking an assurance from Mor that it wouldn't lead them all into trouble.

They no longer had any loyalty to the mainland or the government. For too long they had been ignored and Stack had been starved of investment. Their concerns had never been taken seriously and their fears for the future had been dismissed out of hand by arrogant politicians.

Finally, it was put to the vote and every single person was in favour of Mor's plan.

Mor undertook, along with Alastair MacDonald, to take charge of the operation. It was agreed that a meeting would be held in the hall each week so that they could report on their progress.

Everyone was also sworn to secrecy and made to promise that they would not let mention of it slip during trips to the mainland or when the ferry from the mainland called at the island.

As the meeting drew to a close there remained only one question to be answered.

How the hell were they going to carry out the plan?

"With the help of someone on the mainland," Mor said. "Someone you will all be familiar with."

FIVE

Maclean's plan was diabolically simple.

They'd just go out to the island, load the treasure into a boat, and motor away with it. There were no police officers based on the island and therefore no one to stop them.

Stewart racked his brain for a suitable phrase that could be applied to the task and came up with the brilliantly original saying, 'like taking candy from a baby.'

Maclean said he couldn't see how it could fail to work. He was convinced in fact that it would prove to be the easiest blag any of them had ever pulled.

He revealed that the treasure was stored in a number of suitcases and crates in a house on the island owned by a guy names Ross Mor.

"They took me to see it but I was blindfolded because they didn't want me to know the exact location," he said. "But needless to say I've since found out."

"Just how much treasure is there and how heavy is it?" This from Stewart.

"Most of it is in the form of coins," Maclean said. "There are thousands of them, plus jewellery and other artifacts. So it's not as bulky as you might imagine. I counted three large suitcases and four wooden crates."

"So how come you got involved?" Hodge asked him. "You said you hadn't been back to the island in years."

,

"They approached me out of the blue eight weeks ago," Maclean said. "They knew about the antiques business and they needed someone in the know to help them get rid of the treasure. I fit the bill perfectly. I'm one of them and because of that they trust me. So they offered me a deal and I accepted."

In the beginning Maclean had gone along with Mor's amateurish attempt to cheat the Crown and for a time had actually intended distributing the treasure on their behalf for a modest commission. He was to be given small amounts at a time and had agreed that he would bring the cash to the island after each sale, receiving his fee when it had all been sold.

But it quickly dawned on him that he didn't have to settle for a measly commission. The tight bastards were exploiting his expertise and expecting him to do all the work.

And they assumed he would simply go along with it because he was an islander himself. But they'd been wrong about that.

Although Maclean remembered most of the islanders from his early life on Stack, he no longer regarded himself as one of them. In fact he still looked on his departure at seventeen as the wisest move he had ever made. Not that there had been much for him to stay for, since both his parents had died within a few months of each other. His mother had succumbed to a debilitating cancer and his father to a sudden heart attack.

Indeed, he was thankful now that he had not kept in touch with his old friends and relatives on Stack.

,

Had he done so they might eventually have come to discover that his antiques business was merely a legitimate front for his more lucrative, albeit illegitimate, activities. And then they would never have taken him into their confidence.

Parker was intrigued by the thought of stealing the treasure. But there was one thing that worried him and he decided to raise it with Maclean.

"What about the islanders themselves," he said. "Can we expect them to put up a fight?"

Maclean chuckled. "I hardly think so. Most of them are doddery old men and women. Those that are fit and able enough will melt at the sight of a couple of sawn-offs."

Parker leant forward and examined again the map that Maclean had spread out on the table. It was a three foot square map, courtesy of the Scottish Tourism Board. It showed Stack as a shapeless blob of an island only seven miles long by three miles across.

It had a typical Hebridean landscape. There were cliffs along one side, stretches of sand dunes, large areas of machair, a tiny loch (or lochan) and a small village which had grown up around the tiny harbour with its concrete pier. The highest point on the island was a hill that rose to a mere 400 feet and there were very few trees according to the map.

"Tell me again about their telephone link with the mainland," Parker said.

Maclean smiled. He was pleased that Parker was showing an interest. The Londoner was a solid villain with a good track record. He would be a good man to have on board.

,

"There are only about forty telephones on the island," he explained. "These are served by a small telephone exchange which was recently updated to receive broadband. But it's unmanned and nothing more than a concrete shed. All we've got to do is get inside and fuck up the works. Then the island will be completely cut off. So there's no way they can raise the alarm, even if they want to. It means we'll be long gone before the cops get wind of what's happened."

"Don't the islanders have mobile phones?" Stewart asked.

Maclean shook his head. "That's the beauty of it. There's no reception on Stack. It's been a bone of contention for years but investment has dried up so it's unlikely they'll get a signal for a few years yet."

"How long will they be cut off from the outside world if we disable the telephone exchange?" Parker asked.

"At least a day and a night. The ferries come out from Oban three times a week. So if we do the job, say, late on a Monday there'd be no communication between the mainland and the island until the Wednesday. By then we'd be long gone. That's the beauty of this gig. We get clean away even before they raise the fucking alarm."

"Couldn't they simply cross to the mainland in a boat? There must be some fishing boats out there."

Maclean nodded. "There are three to be exact. I've counted them. But we'll put those out of commission along with the phones."

"So how do we get there and back?"

"We hire our own boat," Maclean said, glancing

,

at Stewart. “That's where Bob comes in. He's a dab hand with boats.”

Parker thought about it some more, then said, “How do we know they won't move the treasure before we get there?”

“I plan to go to the island a day or two earlier with news about the sale of some of their coins. That way I can keep an eye on the stuff, and when you come in after dark I'll be there waiting.”

Parker was impressed by Maclean's thoroughness, but then it had always been one of his trademarks.

“So where exactly do we go in?” he asked.

Maclean leant forward and fingered a point on the map. “That's a disused jetty. I've checked it out and nobody lives near it. We tie the boat there at high tide and leave it unattended. It'll be quite safe.”

“And what happens to the stuff once we've got it?” Parker said.

“We get rid of it straight away,” Maclean said. “The dealers are lined up to take it. They’re based in London. I’ve arranged for transport to take us from Oban.”

“What about afterwards,” Parker said. “The islanders are bound to guess you're the culprit. Won't they be after your blood?”

Maclean shrugged. “They'll have to find me first. I've been planning to sell the business for some time and move on. With the cash from this I can just up and leave. Glasgow and me will be a thing of the past by the time the blag's over.”

Hodge said, “And the most beautiful part of it all is that those twerps out there probably won’t even go screaming to the Old Bill. If they do then they'll have to explain what they were doing with the treasure in the first place."

Maclean went into the other room for some more beers and while he was gone the others remained silent. Each of them went over the plan in his own mind, trying to picture how the raid would happen and what all that treasure would look like. Parker had never been on a blag like it and the idea appealed to his sense of adventure. It seemed like real easy money. There was a low level of risk and little prospect of anyone getting seriously hurt. Jobs like this did not come along very often.

When Maclean came back and was seated, Stewart said, "You haven't told Parker about the girl yet, Andy."

"I was coming to that," Maclean said.

Parker felt his heart skip a beat.

"What's this then?" he asked.

Maclean shrugged as if it wasn't important. "Her name's Bella and she lives on the island. She's an old girlfriend. We had a thing when we were teens and when I went back to the island, well, we got it together again."

"What's she got to do with the blag?"

"I've told her about it."

"You've what?" Parker was stunned. "For Christ's sake man, why?"

"Blimey, Phil, don't split a seam. She's all right. You can take my word for it."

"But I don't get it. Why did she have to know?"

"I needed someone on the inside. I'd forgotten what the place even looked like."

'

"But surely you're on the inside yourself?"

He shook his head. "That's where you're wrong. Like I said, although they were willing to let me get rid of the stuff for them and to see the treasure, they weren't prepared to tell me where it's being kept. That piece of info came from Bella. As well as other useful bits like the disused jetty being there and details about the telephone exchange."

"And she went along with your idea for taking it?"

Parker couldn't believe that this could be so.

"Of course she did."

"But that doesn't make sense," Parker said. "What about her family, friends? They must all live on the island."

"She's single, alone and still in love with me," Maclean said. "She's also desperate to leave the island. So in return for her help I've promised her a new life."

"Jesus," Parker said. "Are you kidding? She could jeopardize the whole frigging operation."

"She won't," Maclean said, his voice high and confident. "She knows exactly what she's getting into and she's up for it. She's been waiting all her life for a chance like this."

Parker frowned and the lines in his forehead bunched tight. "You sure you can trust her?"

"One hundred per cent," Maclean said. "She's besotted with me and I guarantee that she won't let me down."

"So you're actually serious about this lass?" Stewart said.

"Indeed I am," Maclean replied. "In fact I

,

wouldn't be stupid enough to take her into my confidence if I didn't intend to follow through with my promises to her."

There was a long, awkward silence. Maclean sat back in his chair and lit a cigarette. He had a fixed, impenetrable expression on his face.

Eventually, Parker said, "Okay, so we take your word for it that we need the girl and she can be trusted. But no way does she get told our names or anything about us."

"That goes without saying," Maclean said.

Parker looked at the others. They both shrugged.

He issued a long, audible sigh and said, "Now what about weapons? Do you plan for us to go in tooled up?"

"Too bloody right," Hodge piped up. "Put the fear of God in the fuckers right at the start and they won't make trouble."

"Where do we get the pieces?" Stewart asked.

"That'll be my department," Hodge said. "Has anyone any objection to carrying a shotgun?"

There were no objections and Hodge nodded.

"Leave it to me then," he said. "When do you want them by?"

Maclean finished his beer and looked at Parker.

"First of all I have to know if you're in or out, Phil?" he said.

Parker pressed his lips together and thought about it. He liked the set-up, as well as the prospect of getting a share of all that treasure at a time when the price of gold was sky high. His only concern was the girl, but from the sound of it she was an integral part of the package.

,

“Count me in then,” he said finally. “But make sure you keep a tight rein on the girl.”

Maclean grinned. “I knew you'd never turn down a blinder like this in a million years. And don’t fret over Bella. Consider her one of us.”

“So when do we move?” Hodge asked.

Maclean studied his long manicured fingernails for a moment, then looked up. “One week from today,” he said. “That'll give me time to arrange the hire of the boat and fix things up for the immediate distribution of the treasure. We meet in Oban on January fourteen.”

SIX

Oban is everything the guide books say it is, Parker discovered. A town in an enviable position in the Scottish Highlands, overlooking a beautiful bay with a fine view of Kerrera and the mountains of Mull to the west. It is often referred to as the 'Gateway to the Isles' because the famous Caledonian MacBrayne steamers ferry people and cars regularly from there to a number of islands in both the Inner and Outer Hebrides.

In summer the tourists converge and the narrow streets are thronged with garishly dressed adventure seekers, many of whom are weighted down with ridiculously heavy packs containing, among other things, tents, sleeping bags, primus stoves and climbing boots.

Parker was thankful it was January and the town was enjoying a tranquil existence. It was cold but clear which made a change. On his three previous visits to Scotland it had rained incessantly and the sun had failed to make an appearance.

On the last occasion the weather had been so bad that he hadn't left his hotel for two days.

He was enjoying a morning cup of coffee in the restaurant of the hotel on George Street. From the window he could see the quaint little harbour with its crowd of little fishing boats and cantankerous sea birds.

He'd been the first to arrive in the town and he intended hanging around the hotel all day to greet the others when they arrived. He'd been thinking about his accomplices quite a lot during the past week. Maclean, he'd decided, hadn't changed a bit. He was as cunning and as clever as he was three years ago.

But Parker continued to have reservations about the girl, which made him wonder about Maclean's judgement. It was all very well having a contact on the inside, but not best practice to be emotionally involved with that person, as the Scot so obviously was.

Parker had given a lot of thought to this and would most certainly have backed out if it hadn't been for the fact that the job appeared to be such a sure thing. So long as Maclean made sure that the girl didn't blab before the raid then it would be okay. At least that's what he told himself.

Parker had done some checking up on Stewart and it turned out he was a more than competent villain with an impressive record of successes, mostly high end burglaries and hold-ups. According to Parker's contacts Stewart was well respected and well liked within the criminal fraternity both north and south of the border. He was married with three grown-up children and two grand-children.

It was generally assumed that he was now looking for a big score to aid an early retirement. Apparently he was some kind of boat freak and wanted to start up his own charter business abroad.

Hodge was the only one Parker had his doubts about. He didn't like to work with cranks and by all accounts Hodge was a right one for losing his temper. But by the same token he was also known

,

to be a good blagger with a long string of successful jobs to his credit.

Not much was known about the guy's private life, but it was believed he was single and lived by himself in Liverpool. He'd served a three-year stretch in Parkhurst for GBH after causing serious damage to a bloke's face with a glass. The bloke had apparently made the mistake of arguing with him in a pub.

Parker would have preferred to work with someone less volatile, but it wasn't his call. So he sought comfort in the knowledge that this was to all intense and purposes going to be a simple, straightforward raid. Therefore, no reason for Hodge to cause mayhem.

*

At eleven that morning Maclean arrived at the hotel and joined Parker in the bar.

Maclean was dressed to the part of a weekend sailor in white deck shoes and a light blue windcheater. His cheeks were flushed red and his hair was windswept.

Parker ordered him a whisky and when it was poured they sat at a corner table out of earshot of the only other customer in the place.

Maclean said, "You been here long?"

"Few hours."

"So what do you think of the place?"

"Pretty, but boring."

'

Maclean laughed out loud. "The trouble is you're wedded to the big city. The slower pace rankles. I feel the same."

"I suppose you're right," Parker said. "Though I reckon I could get accustomed to it. Life in the smoke is not what it used to be. That's why I fuck off to Spain whenever I can. I have an apartment there. On a golf course."

"Nice for some," Maclean said. Then he looked pensively out the window and when he next spoke his voice was almost a whisper. "You know, I used to think that this town was a huge fucking metropolis. Compared to the island it was. My mum used to bring me here about once a month to do some shopping. It was a big thing in those days to come across to the mainland."

"What was it like living out there?" Parker enquired.

Maclean pulled a face and sipped at his whisky. "For me it was bloody awful. Too cut off from everything. Not enough happening. Looking back on it now the best thing I ever did was leave. The place was killing me."

"Would you have left if your parents hadn't died?" Parker asked.

"Oh, sure. There was no future for me there. At least not one that was particularly appealing. I'd have ended up digging peat bogs for the rest of my life."

They chatted on about inconsequential things for a few minutes and then Parker asked him how things had gone.

Maclean leaned forward and lowered his voice to

,

a steely whisper. "We've got a boat. It's out there in the harbour. There — you can see it through the window."

Maclean pointed. Parker saw a smart white-hulled cabin cruiser that appeared to be making overtures to a small, squat lobster boat moored next to it. Though Parker did not profess to know much about boats, he did think the cruiser would have been more at home on the Norfolk Broads than at sea.

"You sure that will get us there?" he said. "It doesn't look that big to me."

Maclean nodded. "Stewart gave it the once over. He reckons it's okay. There's plenty of room in the cabin and on the decks for the treasure."

"How much is it costing?"

"Couple of grand. I hired it for a week so we'd have it ready and waiting when we decide to go in. And don't worry. It was all organized with a dodgy ID."

"Are we still on for tomorrow?"

Maclean shook his head. "The weather will be against us. They expect gale force winds and rough seas. I don't know about you, but I wouldn't trust Stewart on anything but a dead calm sea."

"That's a pain."

"I agree, but they do forecast better weather on Wednesday. We'll go then."

"Have you been back to the island this past week?" Parker asked.

"I just returned from there. The treasure is still at Mor's place. I had to give Mor five big ones so it looks like I'm making efforts on their behalf. But the good thing is the treasure has already whetted the appetites of the dealers I'm working with. They're having orgasms at the prospect of getting their hands on the rest. From what they're telling me I'm beginning to think we'll get around five million. Maybe more."

Parker whistled through his teeth. "So what would the market value be?" he said.

Maclean shrugged. "It depends how they offload the stuff. They'll want to sell it on without attracting too much publicity. But there'll be plenty of eager buyers. Even if they melt the gold down they'll cover their investment. But the rare artifacts will almost certainly be snapped up by collectors who won't care where they came from. It could push the total haul to well over ten million."

"Wow. So we could be looking at over a million each for a night's work."

Maclean grinned. "Exactly."

Parker swigged back a mouthful of whisky as a bolt of adrenaline rushed through his body.

"So when are you going back to the island?" he asked.

"On Wednesday," Maclean said. "I've told them I'll return soon so they won't be surprised to see me again. I'll go back on the ferry and when you come across later I'll be waiting."

"Has the girl been keeping her trap shut?"

"Like a clam. By the way, you'll be meeting her later. She came over with me."

*

,

They waited in the hotel bar until the other two arrived. Hodge came in from the airport at noon. He looked worn out and it was Parker's guess that the outcome of a hectic night on the booze still tormented him.

He said very little, just listened moodily as Maclean brought him up to date with events. He did express his annoyance, though, when he learned that they would be holding up in Oban for two nights.

“That's something I didn't bank on,” he said.

”Don’t sweat it,” Maclean told him. “We can't help the weather,”

“S'pose not. It's just that I don't like waiting around. It gives me the jitters.”

“Too bad,” Maclean said. “We’ve got no choice. I’ve booked rooms in this place. I’ll open a tab at the bar and we can all sit back and relax. The time will fly past.”

Stewart arrived in the late afternoon by train from Edinburgh. He was still his same gregarious self and bored everyone to tears over drinks with his repertoire of corny jokes about dim Irishmen and tight-fisted Scotsmen.

It was Stewart, however, who made the biggest impression on Bella.

She arrived at six after visiting friends on the outskirts of Oban and was introduced to everyone by Maclean, who was careful not to use their names. Bella was aged about thirty-five and rather attractive in an old fashioned sort of way.

She wore a grey polo sweater under a heavy

,

green anorak. Her jeans were tight and her long, dark hair hung loose about her shoulders.

The guys were wary of her at first and the conversation was stilted. But the drink eventually eased the tension and even allowed Parker to overcome his strong reservations about involving her at all. He actually found himself warming to her. She had a natural charm and a gentle smile. When Hodge came right out and asked her why she was getting involved, she said, "I should have thought that was obvious. I believe that Andy and I were always meant to be together. I let him get away once, but I won't let it happen again. I realize it will mean shedding all ties with the island. But I can live with that. My parents are dead and I have no relatives there. I'll miss my friends but I can make new ones."

It was a good answer and one that impressed Parker. Even so they were careful not to reveal anything about themselves and Bella, shrewdly, didn't ask any difficult questions.

She didn't say much at all in fact, but she did have an awful tendency to laugh insanely at Stewart's wisecracking and this only served to encourage him. All the same, Parker found the afternoon and evening, which was entirely spent in the hotel bar, surprisingly relaxing. And he became aware of an emerging sense of comradeship between the five of them which strengthened his own faith in the venture they were about to embark on.

He also realized something else that evening. It was that Maclean had strong feelings for Bella.

Feelings he was still coming to terms with no doubt. He treated her with total respect and it was also apparent that he was making a conscious effort not to swear in front of her.

Just after ten they decided to call it a day as nobody wanted to wind up drunk. They all retired to their rooms — Bella with Maclean — and it was arranged that they would meet again the next day to look over the cruiser and finalize the plan for relieving the islanders of their new-found wealth.

,

SEVEN

Maclean did not find it easy to go to sleep. Even though he'd exhausted himself by trying to keep pace with Bella, in what had been a rather frantic encounter between two people with an animal craving for each other's flesh, his mind simply refused to be influenced by his weary body. He felt troubled slightly and he couldn't explain the feeling.

Next to him Bella slept fitfully, her long dark hair flung across her chest, her pink pouting lips soft against his left nipple and her breath warm against his skin.

He felt sure she had made a good impression with the guys. She had come across as sincere and committed and very much in love with him. It was a relief for sure, because he had feared that her involvement might have frightened off the ever-cautious Parker.

His mind flashed back through the years and he recalled how he had fancied her something rotten when they were young. She'd been one of only a handful of girls on the island at that time in his own age group. Furthermore, she was the only one who had ever shown any interest in him.

He thought about that unforgettable day all those years ago when she'd struck up an acquaintance with him. She had sat next to him at the back of the only classroom in that tiny island school. At the time, the teacher, an old spinster type with a deep masculine voice, was going on about the history of the islands and trying to instill in their naive minds an appreciation of an ancient culture which even then was in danger of dying out.

Quite out of the blue, Bella, who at fourteen was a freckle-faced kid with a brace on her teeth, placed her right hand in his lap. The gesture caught him completely by surprise. He drew breath sharply, and noisily, causing a few heads to turn.

Bemused and extremely embarrassed, he had simply sat there, the lower half of his body completely numbed by the delightful sensation her hand provoked in his loins. And his face had burned fiercely.

Slowly, and with what he thought must be a practiced hand, she had unzipped him and moved her cold fingers inside his trousers. And he had moaned softly and stared ahead, his mind far removed from the teacher's ramblings. This, he remembered himself thinking at the time, was like nothing else on earth.

She kept her hand there for a full minute and in spite of herself she failed to suppress a giggle when an orgasm caused his knees to shake uncontrollably and the desk to wobble on top of them.

In the months that followed, she pestered him as girls tend to pester the boy they idolize. And, as was only natural, he took advantage of the situation. They eventually became a couple and when he left the island she was devastated. They stayed in touch for a while. She would write to him and he'd phone occasionally. They even had a few wild weekends in Oban, but eight years ago they'd stopped contacting each other. Or rather he had stopped

,

answering her calls and responding to her letters. He'd become too busy and had got involved with another woman.

When Bella learned that he was returning to the island she made a point of being there to welcome him when he got off the ferry. It was rather a poignant reunion and seeing her brought a lump to his throat. What's more he was dumbstruck by the fact that she was still single and living alone.

She was as beautiful as she had always been, with dark brown eyes, high cheekbones and a sensuous mouth.

On the day they were reunited she invited him to her home for a meal. And bombarded him with questions. Was he married? Did he have a serious girlfriend? Any children? Pets? What were his plans for the future? Why had he not stayed in touch? Had he missed her?

Much to his surprise he thoroughly enjoyed the evening. And he had enjoyed answering questions, even the difficult ones. They'd made him feel special. And wanted.

The next day they went for a walk together on the beach and held hands for the first time in years. The day after they made love in the sand dunes. They came together twice and the experience was one that he would savour for the rest of his life. He had never before felt so turned on. So alive. And so comfortable in a woman's arms.

And that was when he realized that his feelings for her were still strong and that he had been a fool to leave her when he did.

He'd never been married himself and his last

’

serious relationship had ended two years ago. Loneliness had crept up on him without him even realizing it and recently he’d begun to view the future with trepidation.

But the fact that Bella still carried a torch for him after all this time convinced him that she was indeed someone special. Someone he should hold on to now that she had come back into his life.

It was that realization that had prompted him to tell her about his audacious plans for the treasure. If she had declined to go along with it then he would have dropped the idea and continued to work with the islanders. But she’d been intrigued and excited at the prospect of a life far removed from the one that she was bored with. And so she’d agreed to help him and that meant there could be no going back on the promises he had made her.

She stirred suddenly beside him and her eyes flickered open. She must have sensed that he was awake.

“Are you no asleep, Andy?” she whispered.

“I'm thinking, love.”

She looked up at him, her liquid green eyes searching his face.

“Is it about this thing you’re going to do?” she asked.

“No. About us. You and me.”

Her eyes opened wider. She pushed herself up on one elbow. Her voice was pleading. “Promise me we'll be together afterwards, Andy. Promise me. Please.”

Without hesitation he smiled, nodding. “I promise, love. Don't you worry. I’ll never leave you

,

again."

"You'd better not," she said. "I won't ever be able to come back."

"You won't have to," he said reassuringly. "From now on your life is with me. We'll go far away from here. We'll get married and have kids. And we'll make up for all those lost years."

Bella snuggled up to him, her flesh soft and warm and he suddenly realized that he was already rich even before he got his hands on his share of the loot.

EIGHT

For once the weather forecasters had been right with their prediction and the evening of the sixteenth was fine. The sky was spotless and the sun strong enough even to penetrate the cold winter atmosphere. Its glow was reflected in a placid sea that looked warm enough to swim in but wasn't. It was a day to delight the sailor. There was a nippy breeze and a gentle swell.

As they cleared Oban harbour, the twin-diesels thudding powerfully beneath them, Stewart was overcome by a feeling of exhilaration. It was a long time since he'd been at the helm of such a fine and expensive craft and he was determined to enjoy the experience even though the object of their mission weighed heavily on his mind.

He was always nervous just before a blag, but he knew that was a good thing. Only fools went into these things with their heads in the clouds.

He reminded himself again of the prize. According to Maclean the treasure was worth millions. So he was banking on his share being more than enough to retire on.

He'd buy that gleaming Princess he had always dreamed of owning someday. Then maybe he'd fuck off to the Med and start a charter business. Or maybe not. Maybe he'd just sit by the pool all day knocking back fancy cocktails.

"Enjoying yourself?" Parker's voice startled him. He'd been miles away.

,

"She's a dilly," he said, with a boyish grin. "Always wanted one like her myself."

"But could never afford her," Parker said. "I know. I've heard it all before."

Stewart took a packet of cigarettes from his pocket and offered one to Parker. They had difficulty lighting them, but managed finally to succeed by cupping their hands around the lighter's flame.

At that moment a gull fluttered down and perched expectantly on the bow. When it realized nothing was being offered, it flew off again, squawking angrily.

"When you reckon we'll get there?" Parker asked.

Stewart drew deeply on his cigarette. The smoke that rose from his lungs was dispersed in a flash by the wind.

"Mac wants us in after dark, so there's no hurry," he said. "We should be there in another hour or so. Just after seven probably."

They had already decided this would be the best time to go in as it would be high tide and they could get close to the jetty provided it wasn't too rough. If it did knock up a bit they'd have to anchor offshore and approach the jetty in the dinghy.

Parker said, "Foresee any problems with this one, Bob?"

Stewart pondered the question. "Not unless The Cowboy gets trigger happy," he said.

Parker frowned. "You think he might?"

"It's happened before," Stewart said. "I thought Mac might have had more sense than to bring him

,

in on this one."

"Why did he?"

"Well, apart from the fact that they've done some jobs together, I suppose he figures Hodge to be a good man." He glanced at the cabin door to make sure it wasn't open so Hodge could hear him. "Don't get me wrong, though. I'm not saying he's some kind of prize prick. It's just that it doesn't take much to make him out someone. Not that I don't hold with killing when it's necessary, you understand. But you know what I mean. He's liable to noise things up by shooting at anything that moves."

It hadn't occurred to Parker that Stewart might also be a bit wary of Hodge, but he was glad in a way. At least it meant that Stewart would also be making sure that the man they called The Cowboy didn't try to live up to his reputation.

"Have you worked with him before?" Parker asked.

Stewart shook his head. "No, but I tend to work north of the border whereas he prefers south. Richer pickings, he says."

Parker nodded. "I gather you've worked with Andy, though?"

"Dozens of times. Good man to have around on a tough'en. He tells me you and him did a few jobs together some years back?"

"That's right."

"Mostly security vans, I gather?"

Parker laughed. "When I think now of the diabolical risks we used to take it's a wonder any of us are still around." He paused, then added, "I suppose that's why I'm so taken by this job. It should be a doddle. I mean, there's hardly any risk attached to it at all."

Stewart grinned. "Watch what you're saying, old mate. You must know yourself it's usually on the simple jobs you come a cropper."

*

Precisely ten minutes after seven they arrived at the island.

Thanks to Maclean, who was there swinging a torch to and fro, they were able to pin-point the exact position of the jetty from offshore. Left to their own devices, they would never have found it in the pitch dark.

There were no lights on this side of the island. Most of the crofts and houses were concentrated around the pier and on the west side. According to the map, this side of the island was given over mainly to open moorland with a scattering of those ubiquitous derelict 'black houses' that were once occupied by large crofting families and were now grim reminders of a dying age.

Their arrival was without incident. Stewart maneuvered the boat deftly into a small cove and between a group of half submerged rocks.

Then they were up against the weed-covered timbers of the tumbledown jetty. The water was rougher here, waves running about three feet from crest to trough, and there were some hairy moments as they tried to get the mooring line across to Maclean.

The boat heaved and dived, heaved and dived, and without adequate fenders the hull scraped dangerously against the pilings. But eventually Maclean had the lines secured and the slack was taken in so the boat had less of a tendency to pitch.

When the engine was turned off all that could be heard, aside from the howling wind, was the tide gurgling over the rocks and the soft kissing sound of water being sucked into little clefts and gullies.

The rocks stretched away into the night on either side of them and Parker wondered what had ever possessed the islanders to place the jetty in such an awkward and dangerous position. It was no wonder they no longer used it, he thought.

"Everything okay?" Maclean called out.

"Right as rain," Stewart replied. "You?"

"Raring to go."

"Any hitches?"

"Not so far."

Stewart and Parker lowered themselves on to the jetty and Parker spoke to Maclean. "So where is the treasure?"

"Still at Mor's house. I've borrowed a van. It's plenty big enough to carry the treasure. It's up the hill on the road."

"What about the fishing boats?"

"All three have gone to bed in the harbour," Maclean said.

Hodge jumped down on to the jetty and handed round the shotguns. Parker took a ball of four nylon stockings from his pocket and handed those out, too.

Hodge pulled a face. "Are these really

,

necessary?"

"It's best to be on the safe side," Maclean told him. "You probably won't even have to wear it as I doubt you'll see anyone."

Hodge accepted his stocking with a measure of reluctance and stuffed it into the side pocket of his anorak.

A moment later all four were standing in a huddled group on the jetty. Around them the wind was brewing, moaning plaintively in the darkness like a dog lamenting the death of its beloved owner.

The night was no longer such an impenetrable shroud. Their eyes had grown accustomed to it and vague black outlines were beginning to take on a distinctive form. A hill rising like a pyramid into the clouds, the chimney of a derelict 'black house', and what looked like steps hewn out of bare rock climbing upwards from the jetty, over-grown with weeds and heather.

"I ask you," Hodge whispered. "Who in his right mind would want to live up here?"

Stewart felt uneasy, too. "Well, come on," he said. "Let's get on with it. Nothing's going to get done if we stand around here scratching ourselves."

"Right," Maclean said. "But let's run quickly through the plan. First we go to the harbour where you, Bob, disable the fishing boats. And don't hang about. Just wrench out a few necessary parts. We then drive up to the telephone exchange where you two" — he gestured towards Stewart and Hodge — "mess up the equipment. It's not manned so you shouldn't have any trouble there. Meanwhile, Parker and I will go on to Mor's house and load the

,

treasure into the van. We'll pick you up on the way back. I drop you off back here and while you load the treasure I go and pick up Bella from her house. In all it should only take an hour and a half from start to finish. Then it's back here and we're on our way."

Maclean looked at each of them.

"Any questions?" he said. There were none. "Then let's go."

They trundled up the steps and found a large Bedford van parked on the narrow road at the top of the hill. Its tyres were caked in dry mud and there was writing on the side that was indecipherable under the grime. Here the wind was stronger and Stewart began to have some misgivings about the weather.

Looking up at the sky, he said, "If this gets any worse it could make things bloody difficult on the way back."

"A storm wasn't forecast," Maclean pointed out.

"You don't have to tell me that," Stewart said, his Scottish accent more pronounced than usual. "But that doesn't mean we won't have one. Look at that sky. Not a frigging break in the cloud. And this wind. I tell you I don't like it."

"Quit worrying," Maclean told him. "It's too late to turn back now anyway. Let's worry about how to get back once we have the treasure."

Stewart shrugged his shoulders and followed the others into the van. Maclean and Parker shared the front seat and Hodge and Stewart crouched in the back on the dust-covered floor.

When the headlamps were switched on they

,

poured light over a shabby road of weathered bitumen that was fringed by desolate moorland. It was an inhospitable sight. Stark and lonely.

"Are we likely to bump into anyone?" Parker asked, thinking it distinctly unlikely.

"Not at this time of the evening," Maclean assured him. "Mid-week, people usually go to bed double early. And believe me, they need to after the kind of work these people put into the average day."

The engine spluttered into life and the van jogged off along the road. Suddenly, the moon appeared through a gap in the cloud cover, spilling a pale wintry glow over the stark, undulating wilderness. At the roadside were a couple of abandoned crofts and ruined byres — silent witness to a vanished population. Beyond them, rising into the night, heather-covered hills around which were spread bleak shaggy moors. Occasionally a light would show, a mere pin prick in the darkness, and it would serve as a chilling reminder of their isolation.

The road was rutted and sinuous and only a short step up from being a cart track.

It took them all of ten minutes to get to the island's capital, which was nothing more than a cluster of small two-storey grey houses strung out along either side of the poorly surfaced road. This one street alone, according to Maclean, constituted the entire village. There was a grocer's, a post-office, a church. Out of about twenty houses only eight were showing light.

The street was completely deserted, and the silence, when they stopped briefly to look around, was almost palpable. An air of peace and

,

permanence hung over the place like a heavy blanket. All the houses were matchbox size, rather quaint, and there was no escaping the fact that the place possessed a charm all its own.

The van crept slowly along the road and turned left on its squeaky axle on to a narrow earth road between two houses. This took them down to the harbour where three small fishing vessels bounced at their moorings and a few rowing boats were drawn up on a small shingle beach.

"They should be easy enough to disable," Stewart said. "They run on diesels and I've worked on those often enough."

Hodge said, "You told us there were only three boats, Mac. I can see at least six."

"We've only got to concern ourselves with the fishing boats," Maclean said. "The other boats are only for use around the island. They wouldn't attempt to cross to the mainland in one of those."

As the van journeyed on to the concrete pier the four of them studied the shadows in silence. Although Maclean was not surprised to find the place entirely devoid of life, the others were. It was as if they were the only people on the island, cut off from the rest of civilisation.

The fishing boats were moored in a line along the pier. Maclean pulled up next to the first one and switched off the engine. Again the heavy silence closed in on them.

He gestured towards the boats and spoke softly. "They're all yours, Bob. Make it quick. If anyone comes along I'll whistle a warning. Okay?"

"Okay."

Stewart beamed a smile at the others, picked up the small canvas bag containing the tools he had purchased in Oban, and lowered himself down the iron ladder on to the boat's deck. As he set to work on the engine the others climbed out and had a smoke as they listened to the clanging of metal on the deck below.

The bitter wind lashed unmercifully at their faces and as Parker looked down into the blackened water of the harbour it was as if it was beginning to boil before his very eyes.

Turning to the others, he said, “It'll be hell going back.”

For the first time, Maclean's face betrayed his concern. “Don't worry. We'll be all right.”

“I only hope Stewpot is as good a sailor as he's cracked up to be,” Hodge said. “Because I never did learn to swim.”

Stewart spent about ten minutes on each boat and in all that time no one came to enquire what they were up to.

When Stewart's work was done, Maclean said, “You were quick.”

“They were a piece of cake. I only had to undo a few nuts and screws.”

“You're sure they won't be able to use the boats tomorrow?”

“Well, let's put it this way,” he said, smiling mischievously. “If they want to, they'll have to find the parts first — and I threw those over the side.”

They piled into the van and backed off the pier on low revs. Minutes later they were outside a small brick-built hut just up the road from the village.

,

According to Maclean it was typical of the many exchanges located on islands throughout the Hebrides.

Maclean stopped the van. "This is the exchange. Parker and I have to follow the road for about a mile to Mor's place. We'll see you back here in about forty five minutes."

Stewart and Hodge walked up to the heavy wooden door, each carrying a shotgun and a crowbar insulated with rubber. As they set about forcing the door open, Maclean drove off.

,

NINE

Ross Mor removed the pipe from his mouth and looked up at his daughter as she entered the room. Her shoulder length hair was tucked up under a flowered headscarf and she was wearing a thick beige duffle-coat. As she walked across the tiny room, full of rustic furniture and the memories of happier times, the orange glow of the open fire stroked her cheeks. She leaned over her father and kissed him affectionately on the forehead.

"I'll not be late, dad. I promise."

Anna was going down to the village to spend the evening with Kate Ruag. They'd probably have supper together and gossip over a game of draughts. Mor smiled up at her. He was thankful that he didn't have to fear for her safety whatever time she went out. On the mainland he'd be worried sick if he knew she was going to walk across desolate moorland in the pitch dark. But here on Stack he knew she was in no danger at all.

"Enjoy yourself, lassie," he said. "And be sure to bring me back a piece of Morag's fine cake, you hear?"

"I shan't forget. Now, will you be wanting a cup of tea before I go?"

"Ach, no, lassie. I'll do myself some hot chocolate shortly and then I'll be off to bed."

,

As he turned his head to gaze pensively into the crackling fire, Anna felt a twinge of pity for him. Her mother's death had hit him hard. He was still drowning in grief and there was nothing she could do about it except to be there for him.

She was tempted for a moment to kneel at his feet and offer words of comfort, but she had done that so many times during the past five months and rarely did it make him feel any better. If anything it only made him worse. Enhanced his sense of loss.

She said, "Would you rather I stayed with you tonight? I wouldn't mind, truly. 'Tis an awful night out anyway."

Her words pulled him back to the present. He sucked thoughtfully on his pipe and forced another smile.

"No, you go out and enjoy yourself. I'll be all right. I've got some thinking to do."

"About the treasure, I'll bet."

When he nodded, she cheered up slightly. At least, she thought, this treasure business was keeping his mind occupied for some of the time.

"I'm calling a meeting for tomorrow night," he said. "So I can report on what progress we've made."

"And what progress have you made so far?" she asked him.

"Well, young Maclean has been doing like we asked him. Already he's raised over five thousand pounds for us and only a few coins and trinkets have been sold at that."

"And what is to be done with the money?" She knew very well what was to be done with it, but she wanted him to know she was interested.

"It's going into a kitty, lassie. And when we've sold everything we'll start putting it to good use."

Anna stared into his eyes for a long moment, wishing to God that her mother could be here to share this new adventure with him.

"Best you be going," he told her, breaking her train of thought. "The torch is over there on the shelf."

Once outside the tiny cottage Anna pulled up the collar of her coat and bowed her head into the wind. She felt guilty suddenly for having left her father to spend the evening alone, but even if she did turn back now she knew he would only be upset by her show of sympathy.

So she closed the front gate behind her and with the beam of the torch dancing crazily on the surface of the road, she hurried down the hill towards the village.

She had gone about half way when she saw the blazing headlights of a car coming towards her. Briefly she wondered who it could be. She stepped to the side of the road to let it pass and when it drew level she leaned forward and tried to catch a glimpse of the occupants.

The driver turned his head towards her, and unmistakably it was Andrew Maclean. She raised her hand to wave but before the gesture could be carried through the van was already past her. She resumed her walking, feeling happier in the knowledge that her father would shortly be having some company.

*

Five minutes after Anna had left there was a knock at the door. Ross Mor immediately assumed his daughter had returned, probably because she'd forgotten something. He dragged himself up from his fireside chair, placing his pipe in the ashtray on the table, and went to answer it.

He turned the knob and the door threw itself open.

Two men barged in. He felt a hand slam against his chest, shoving him backwards into the living room.

His features froze in an attitude of disbelief as he stared from one to the other. He couldn't see their faces because they were wearing masks. But they were big and threatening and he knew they were strangers.

For a second he thought he was losing his grip on reality. I must be seeing things, he thought. A dream. No, a nightmare. It has to be. These two hideous creatures can only be visions of a tired mind. Nothing more.

But as realization dawned so the adrenaline of fear paralysed his body, freezing his flesh and numbing his senses. He found he could no longer move, not even to turn and run, as the two men came further into his home, slamming the door behind them.

,

They were shouting out words that didn't register with him and their guns were cocked in a threatening manner.

He fell against the wall cabinet, knocking over glasses and plates.

And then they were coming at him from both the right and left. He heard himself cry out.

But a second later a sharp pain lanced through the back of his skull and he felt himself falling forward into a black, pain-filled void.

,

TEN

They saw the beam of the torch coming down the road towards them, probing the darkness like an accusing finger. They'd just finished their business in the hut where they had ruined the island's entire communications system in an orgy of mindless destruction, and were standing outside waiting for the others to return.

They concealed themselves behind the hut and had waited in unbearable silence for whoever it was to pass them by.

But then they heard a girl's voice. She was singing to herself, a soft gentle sound broken up by the wind.

Hodge glanced conspiratorially at Stewart and nodded in the girl's direction. She was now drawing level with them.

"I reckon we should make the most of this," he said. "Let's have a bit of fun."

"Are you fucking crazy?" Stewart said.

Hodge shrugged. "She's by herself and there's nothing to stop us seizing an opportunity."

Stewart shook his head, "Don't be a fool. The others will be back at any minute."

"Sod the others. Besides, they might be ages yet. We can pass the time any way we please now we've done the job."

"But what if ..."

Hodge sprang to his feet.

,

"Oh, come on, Stewpot. Anybody would think she was your own fucking daughter."

*

Anna was shocked when the figure stepped out from behind the exchange. She raised the torch and aimed it.

The light revealed a tall, good-looking man, with dark, wind-blown hair and squinting eyes. She knew immediately that he was a stranger and sensed just as quickly that there was something bad about him. She'd never seen him before and had heard no mention of such a man being on the island. Her heart began to beat faster and her hands trembled slightly.

"Hello there, young lady," the man called out. "Lost, are you?"

She didn't answer. She couldn't summon the nerve to speak.

Slowly, the man walked towards her. Beyond him, she noticed now, there was another man, smaller and plumper, and he, too, was walking towards her.

Her natural instincts told her to drop the torch and run, that these men were not friendly. But for some reason she couldn't. She found she could only stand there as if the very soles of her boots were glued to the road. Fear and shock had conspired to produce this reaction in her.

"Out for walkies are we?" the first man said,

,

grinning.

Anna realized suddenly that something dreadful was going to happen to her. The man was smiling, teeth glowing white in the torch's beam, but there was no warmth in his smile. As his cold, malevolent eyes looked her up and down there was a kind of predatory glint in them.

"I'm not going to hurt you," he said, not very convincingly.

"Wh ... who are you?" she managed weakly.

As he got to within a couple of feet of her she lowered her right arm and the light fell from his face to form a bright pool at his feet. In the darkness his voice was even more frightening.

"At the moment, little girl, we're strangers. But when it's over you'll probably know me better than any man alive."

All at once she knew what he meant and panic overcame her. She dropped the torch and the bulb went out as it crashed to the ground.

But she had left it too late. There was no escape, not now. Big strong hands latched on to her shoulders as she turned to run. Then he increased the pressure and she screamed with pain and fear as he forced her to her knees.

"Now we're going to have some fun, Stewpot," the man called over his shoulder. "Come on. Help me get her off the road."

*

Stewart stepped forward hesitantly and stared

down at the helpless wretch of a girl. She was screaming, struggling wildly, but her efforts proved fruitless. Hodge placed his hands under her armpits and started dragging her towards the heather.

She was wearing a thick tweed skirt without tights and as the hem got caught on a stone the material tore, revealing a smooth white thigh.

It caught Hodge's eye, and he laughed wickedly. Then he let go of one of her arms and reached forward to make the tear bigger. This time the material split all the way to her waist, revealing a pair of clinging white panties with a cute teddy bear motif.

"What a lovely sight," Hodge bellowed. "Come on, Stewpot. Put some effort into it for fuck's sake. I want mine before the others get here."

Stewart was caught up in the excitement of the moment. Although fully aware that what they were doing was despicable, he couldn't stop himself going along with it.

Later, he knew, he'd feel desperately ashamed of himself, but he also knew it was something he could live with. After all, it wouldn't be the first time he had forced himself on a woman.

He stooped to take hold of her kicking feet and together they carried her off the road on to the moor. Her screams were carried away on the wind and her struggling eased off a little through exhaustion.

They dropped her on her back in the heather and Hodge stood astride her, looking down into her terrified face, his own face glowing with a crude satisfaction.

“I'm going to screw the arse off you,” he announced hoarsely. “And you'll love every minute of it. I promise.”

As Hodge began to feverishly rip off her clothes, Stewart became aware of his own bulging erection and he found himself praying that Parker and Maclean wouldn't get back before he'd had his turn with the girl.

“Look at these tits,” Hodge cried out ecstatically. “They're beauts.”

The girl was almost naked now. Only shreds of clothing clung to her arms and legs. But she was still squirming and screaming, trying to scratch and punch her attacker whenever he was forced to release one or both her hands.

“Hold her while I get my trousers off.”

Stewart sat astride the girl to hold her down. He wasn't as rough as Hodge had been. He tried not to hurt her, and in a ridiculous attempt to calm her told her that if she would just let herself go it would all be over in a few minutes.

When Hodge was free of his trousers and underpants, he pushed Stewart out of the way and fell on top of the girl, pulling her legs apart as he did so. He tried to force himself into her but found he couldn't because she was moving about too much.

“Keep still, you stupid bitch,” he yelled.

But the girl would not give in. She thrust her hips from left to right, up and down, crying, screaming, spitting into his seething face.

Finally, Hodge could take no more of it. He

,

slapped her twice, hard. "Now, be still."

As he fell forward a second time, though, he made the mistake of loosening his grip on her right arm. She lifted it with the speed of a striking cobra and thrust two sharp fingernails deep into his left eye.

He let out a deafening howl and rolled off her, clawing at his injured eye. When he took his hand away to look there was no blood, but the pain was abominable. He stared down at the girl, oblivious to the fact that Stewart was urging him to forget it and to lock her up in the hut.

He leant forward and lifted her to her feet by her hair.

His anger was manic, uncontrolled. He threw his clenched fist into her soft, flat stomach, and his knee he brought up hard between her legs. She cried out and fell to the ground.

Then he knelt beside her and began to punch. And punch.

And punch.

Stewart was horrified. He turned away. He simply couldn't bear to look and didn't dare try to stop Hodge, who was like a crazed animal attacking a still-warm carcass.

The girl was no longer screaming. Her body was no longer white where the blood from her face had splattered in all directions. Suddenly she was limp, like a rag doll, but he continued to beat frenziedly at her lifeless flesh. His eyes were wide, containing a savage glint, and bile dribbled from the corners of his mouth.

When he did finally stop, after about a

,

minute, he gazed in wonder at his hands as if they had acted of their own accord.

*

Sweat glistened on Hodge's forehead as he stood at the side of the road waiting for the van's lights to show at the crest of the hill. He was trembling under his clothes and it wasn't because of the cold. Stewart was standing next to him, pale faced, his shotgun at his feet. He, too, was unable to stop himself from shaking. There was an air of fearful apprehension about the two men which came very close to being tangible in the cold night air.

Stewart was near to breaking point. His mind was a shamble of senseless thoughts and boiling emotions. Hodge, on the other hand, was far less influenced by emotion. He was reacting to an intense physical sensation which he had experienced exactly five minutes earlier and from which his muscles still vibrated.

Stewart turned his head towards Hodge and there was hatred in his eyes. A deep intense hatred that the other could almost feel.

"Did you have to do that?" Stewart cried out.

"Shut up and let me think."

"But you're insane. A fucking madman."

Hodge reacted violently this time, viciously swinging the butt of the shotgun into Stewart's stomach. The blow caused the paunchy Scot to double over and drop to one knee.

,

Hodge took a step forward, raised the shotgun above his head threateningly.

"Do you want some more of the same?"

Stewart lifted his right arm in a feebly defensive gesture.

"That's enough," he pleaded. "No more."

"Then shut the fuck up."

Clutching his stomach, Stewart got to his feet. As he paused to catch his breath he contemplated going for his own gun, but discarded the idea immediately. He was forced to admit that in a confrontation of this nature he was no match for a cold-blooded bastard like Hodge.

He turned and looked at the patch of heather not five yards away which barely concealed the girl's body.

"What are we going to do?"

Hodge turned on him, the whites of his bulging eyes like bright stars in the darkness.

"We just leave her there, you idiot. What do you think?"

"But she'll be found."

"What does it matter? No one will come across here until tomorrow and by then we'll be far away."

Stewart groped for words. "But it'll mean they'll have to call in the Old Bill now for certain."

"So what? They don't know any of us from Adam."

"They know Mac."

"That's his worry."

"You're a heartless bugger."

,

Hodge forced out a mirthless clap of laughter. "Ain't we all? Yes, even you, Stewpot, or have you forgotten already your own part in it?"

This remark really hit the mark. It caused Stewart to catch his breath. His insides wound themselves up into a tight ball and a prickly hand crawled up his spine, touching the raw nerves.

This was something he hadn't yet considered. His own involvement in the atrocity. There could be no denying that he himself was almost as culpable as Hodge. After all, hadn't he just stood by and watched it happen.

Twin lights pierced the darkness at the top of the hill. Grew larger as they came nearer.

Hodge drew breath sharply, looked at Stewart. "If you know what's good for you, Stewpot, you'll keep your mouth shut about what's happened."

"You don't have to tell me that," Stewart said, bending to pick up his shotgun. "It's one thing to have to live with what I've done and something else to broadcast it."

"That's sensible."

"Not that they won't find out. There's no way that the police won't get wind of it now."

Hodge shrugged and spat at the ground. "Too bloody bad."

When the van stopped, Parker's face looked up at them through the half-open window.

"Back's open. Get in."

They climbed in and were immediately awed by the presence of the suitcases and wooden crates that were piled up in the back.

"Why not take a look," Maclean said, when they

,

were settled and the van was on its way. "They're not locked."

Stewart opened one of the cases. A pile of gold and silver coins shone dully in the poor light. There were also gold rings, a silver plate and lots more besides. He reached his hand in and scooped up a dozen or so coins.

"As Bob said back in Glasgow," Parker put in. "It was like taking candy from a baby. The old feller didn't even know what hit him."

"How did it go?" Maclean asked.

"Sweet as a nut," Hodge said. "We clobbered that place but good. They won't be making any calls to the mainland for a while."

"No problems?"

There was just a split second's hesitation before Hodge replied, but it went unnoticed.

"None," he said.

"So you didn't see the girl?" Maclean said.

Stewart froze. "Girl! What girl?"

"Ross Mor's daughter. We passed her on the road. I thought she'd pass you. She must have been going to the village. I'm not sure if she recognized me or not. Still, not that it matters now anyway."

"We didn't see any girl," Hodge offered, just a little too quickly.

Stewart began to breathe again and Hodge winked at him.

"So far so good then," Maclean said after a moment. "And we're nearly home and dry already." He looked over his shoulder. "What d'you think of this weather, Bob? Anything to worry about?"

,

"Eh ..." Stewart came out of himself with a start. He looked beyond Parker's shoulder and frowned at the windscreen. "I didn't realize it was so bad."

The wind from the Atlantic had built up considerably and was strong enough now to cause the van to rattle on its springs. The long slender grass at the roadside yielded in its path and clumps of birch fled across the moors in front of them.

"Provided we get under way soon we should be okay," Stewart hazarded. "The cruiser is big enough to take on a storm this size. If it does get really wild out there I'll take her in close to Mull. We could even hold up in one of the bays until the worst of it is over."

The road back to the disused jetty was as dark and deserted as it had been on the way up. As they passed again through the village they saw that only three of the houses were now showing light.

They came to the hill above the jetty and stopped the van. Parker climbed out and went to the rear to open the doors. Stewart jumped down first and crossed the road to take a look down the hill at the boat.

He stared for about thirty seconds, allowing his eyes to become accustomed to the darkness because he wasn't sure he was seeing correct, and then he turned to the others and announced in a voice that was remarkably calm, "She's gone. The bloody boat's gone."

,

ELEVEN

The lethal combination of wind and rough sea had torn the boat from her mooring. The rope knots had come loose under pressure.

From the top of the hill they could see no sign of the boat and they assumed she had been dragged out to sea on receding waves or sucked under after smashing her hull on the side of the jetty. But then they saw that the cruiser was actually riding the waves not fifty yards out, rearing up on every breaking swell like a frightened mare at barbed wire.

She was going to hit those half submerged rocks. They could all see it coming. And there wasn't a damn thing any of them could do to stop it happening.

The wind howled, cursed, screamed.

Four helpless figures stood staring forlornly into the night. The sea, bursting against the jetty, soaked their clothes, their hair, their faces.

Ca-rash.

The sound of the hull being torn on the jagged rocks. Rising above the wind. A sound like a house being crushed under a giant's foot.

Grrrrraaagh.

Bits of white scattered the gloom. The bow shot upwards, turned full circle, came down to shatter on rock only a few inches below the surface.

,

A second later the boat was upended, pointing accusingly at the sky, and then, slowly, it began to disappear in a swirling cloud of foam and spray.

And that was it.

The four men stood staring at the water. Hypnotised. Soaking wet and not caring.

A long time passed before anyone spoke. It was Parker, and his words were barely discernible.

"That's our fucking lot," he said.

Stewart was aghast. His head swivelled towards Parker, his face dripping, and his mouth fell open. He didn't say anything. But then what could he say that needed to be said? That one short sentence spelled out the hopeless situation facing them. With the boat gone they were without a means of escape.

Parker's mind recoiled from the shock and he was suddenly aware that they were marooned. Short of swimming all those miles to the mainland, there was no way off the island.

He and Maclean stood with their backs against the side of the van, faces glum. Hodge was in front of them and Stewart sat cross-legged on the damp ground, his face buried in his hands.

They remained like that for several minutes, then Hodge lunged forward suddenly, grabbing Maclean by the front of his anorak.

"You fucking idiot," he yelled into his face. "This is all your fault. You must have left the knots loose. Now we've all had it."

Maclean made no attempt to push Hodge away. It was as if he had been drained of all energy and emotion. He just stood there, blank-faced, allowing Hodge to shake and threaten him like a madman.

,

Finally, Parker felt constrained to intervene and broke them apart.

"Now, hold on," he yelled. "Fighting's not going to get us anywhere."

Hodge, his face suffused with anger, stepped back and thrust a finger at Maclean, who was watching him through vacant eyes.

"Because of that silly bleeder, we haven't got a prayer. A bloody van full of treasure and we can't go anywhere with it."

Parker could well understand Hodge's anger, and indeed he shared it, but he couldn't see that rubbing it in Maclean's face would serve any useful purpose now.

"We need to keep it together," Parker said. "And then work up a way to get out of this."

"So what have you got in mind?" Hodge spat the words. "They've got us by the cobblers and you know it."

"What about those boats we saw?" Parker said. "Maybe we can rig one up with an outboard motor and get to Mull, even in these conditions. If not, at least we'll have it handy for when the weather improves."

"And what if there is no outboard engine?" Hodge growled.

Parker shrugged. "Then we'll just have to give the treasure back and try to talk the islanders out of going to the police. I don't see what else we can do."

"And supposing they don't take it so lightly? Supposing they don't let us leave?"

"We still have the shotguns," Parker

reminded him. "We'll just have to hang around until we can fix up a boat or until the ferry comes across from the mainland. Don't forget they still won't want the authorities to know about the treasure."

There was a heavy silence between them which lasted several seconds. Then Stewart got to his feet and said, "There's no way these people are going to let us leave here without paying for what we've done."

"Oh, come off it," Parker said. "They can live with it. Granted, we had to clobber the goon at the house, but he'll survive."

"I'm not thinking about him," Stewart said, switching his irate gaze to Hodge. "I'm thinking about the girl."

Hodge flew at Stewart, grabbing him by the throat, and yelling for him to keep his mouth shut. It took both the others to pull him off. As they held onto him he continued to stare at Stewart, his eyes cold and fanatical.

"Go on," Parker said. "Tell us about the girl."

*

"Then she's dead," Parker said incredulously, after hearing what Stewart had to say. "You've fucking murdered her!"

Stewart poked a rigid finger at Hodge.

"He murdered her. Not me. I tell you I've never seen anything like it. The man's a ruddy psycho."

,

As Hodge tried to struggle free Parker let go of his arm and smacked a fist into his face.

Hodge reeled backwards, lost his footing, and fell sprawling to the ground.

He was quick to recover, though, and came back at Parker with a tiger's speed. But Parker had already retrieved the shotgun and as Hodge got to within arm's length he let fly with the barrel, which landed with a heavy thud on the other's chest.

Hodge was still gasping for breath as Parker sent the butt crashing into his stomach. This time Hodge went down and was in no hurry to get up. He turned on his back, clutching his stomach, and looked up.

Parker stood over him, panting, trying hard to contain his rage. "Until this is over I'll put up with you," he seethed. "But afterwards you'd better watch your back, because the first chance I get I'm going to make you regret ever having been born."

Parker braced himself for an attack which didn't come.

Hodge stayed where he was, started to reply and thought better of it. He let his eyes carry the message that told Parker, in no uncertain terms, that he, too, had better watch his back from now on.

Parker took a deep breath and turned away from him.

"For now we'll forget about what's happened and concentrate on getting off the island. I suggest we go down to the village right now and see if we can find an outboard engine or something. If there aren't

,

any, maybe we can get one of the fishing boats going."

Stewart shook his head. "No way. We'd need all the parts for that, and they're in the sea."

"Then we'll just have to go down and get them, won't we?" Parker said irritably. "Because if we don't get away from this place before morning, we'll never get away."

,

TWELVE

There was a blackness in front of his eyes that began to slowly break up like a jig-saw being dismantled piece by piece. At first, light just trickled through in small doses, revealing blurred images of an assortment of objects around him. Gradually these objects came into focus. The stout, glossy legs of a highly polished table, a stone fire-place and a threadbare rug on the floor with its ends curling inwards.

Eventually his vision widened enough to embrace an entire room that seemed to be lying on its side. He realized it was his room, the familiar belongings of a lifetime about him. And suddenly he remembered with startling clarity what had happened and why it wasn't the right way up.

Ross Mor pushed himself up on one elbow and winced at the explosion of pain inside his head. He clamped his eyes shut and touched his forehead with a surgeon's gentleness. There was a nasty bump and an open wound that wet the tips of his fingers with blood. His first instinctive thought was to go into the bathroom and apply a dressing to it, but he decided there were more important things to do first. Like finding out what the hell was going on.

It took all his strength to raise himself to his feet. He staggered into the bedroom like a drunk trying to find his way around a strange house.

He hadn't expected the treasure to be there in the

,

back room, so he wasn't surprised to see that it was gone. The bastards who had stormed his house had taken it. They were robbers, looters, wild beasts.

He leaned against the door frame and rubbed his knuckles into his eyes to eradicate the pain behind them. But it did no good. He turned back into the living room and dropped into his worn-out armchair by the fire. The smell of burning peat filled the room and his nostrils. He glanced over his shoulder at the door. At least they'd had the decency to close it behind them, he thought.

He laid his head back and stared bleary-eyed at the ceiling. There was no point trying to apply careful thought to the situation at this moment. He wasn't up to it. His mind was in no fit state to grapple with anything but the very basic questions like who they were and where had they gone? Any attempt to examine the facts in closer detail only caused his head to hurt even more and he had no wish to inflict further punishment upon himself.

Even so, several things were obvious. There had been two men — or at least he had seen two men — and they had been strangers. He was certain of that even though they had worn masks and had hardly spoken. You don't live in a small island community all your life and not get to know everyone as well as you know your own family.

The mantelpiece clock told him he had only been unconscious for about half an hour. Perhaps there was still time to stop them leaving the island, which would obviously be their intention.

He picked up his phone to raise the alarm, only

to find that he had no dialing tone. Shit. What now?

He got up, pulled on his overcoat and boots, and hurried out of the cottage. He decided not to cut across the moors as they were probably waterlogged, which would slow him down, so he began running down the road, the wind blasting his face. He stumbled twice in the dark, but otherwise was making fairly good time all things considered.

He came to the tiny automatic telephone exchange and pulled up sharply when he saw that the wind was whipping the door back and forth on its squeaky hinges. He left the road to investigate, though in his mind he had an idea what to expect. If the door was open then somebody must have forced it.

And he was right. The inside was a shambles. Torn out wires were strewn across the floor and the flimsy metal that encased the expensive looking machinery had been battered into unrecognisable heaps of junk. Unquestionably the gangsters had planned their raid well. They had been very efficient and, yes, clever. He wondered fleetingly how they had found out about the treasure and Andrew Maclean immediately sprang to mind.

Perhaps he had passed the information on to one of his mainland contacts and the wrong people had got to know of it. He was certain that Maclean himself would not have been involved. After all, he was an island lad, and therefore completely trustworthy. And besides, he hadn't even known where the treasure was hidden.

On the other hand, it was also possible that one of the islanders had unwittingly given the information

,

to some rascal in Oban, who had got a group of lads together and hired a boat. The possibilities as to how these men had found out about the treasure were too numerous to ponder right now, so he shut the door and trudged back to the road.

His right shoe kicked against something tinny and he bent to pick it up.

A torch.

A hand clawed at his heart and pulled it up into his throat. He stared at the object for what amounted to seconds, hoping it would disappear suddenly or turn into a stick or a rock. The glass was smashed, along with the bulb inside, so obviously Anna had dropped it.

But why had she dropped it? And where was she now? At first, his mind refused to accept the obvious, which was that she had been attacked by those same two men. He wanted to believe that she had dropped the torch accidentally and, failing to find it in the dark, had simply gone on to the village. Nevertheless he looked around.

It didn't take him long to find her and he was thankful in a way that it was dark because he knew it spared him the real horror of what lay there in the heather.

He could see enough to know she was almost naked and covered in blood. But the blood was not red. The night turned it into a ghastly collection of inky stains on her pale flesh. Whoever had done this was an animal. A monster. Anna was barely recognizable. Her lips were swollen and torn and her nose was just an unsightly smudge between her wide staring eyes.

“Oh, my God, what have they done to you, lassie?”

Touching her cold flesh brought emotion to the surface in a sudden, surging flood, and he collapsed on top of her, crying uncontrollably. It began to drizzle and the thunderous wind blew the rain on to the back of his neck and began to wash away the blood from Anna's face.

He would have gone on crying for much longer if the hate hadn't welled up in him suddenly. It overcame his grief for a brief moment and made him think of his daughter in a curiously detached way. He looked down at her, tears streaming down his cheeks, and he knew he would have to punish the men who had done this, if not for Anna's sake, then for his own.

He pushed himself to his feet, slipped out of his coat, and wrapped it gently around his daughter. Then he lifted her in his arms and started walking towards the village.

THIRTEEN

There were only five street lamps in the village. One of them was situated outside the tiny post office where Ross Mor came to a stop.

Anna's left arm was hanging limp and as it swung from side to side in a wide arc its shadow grew out of all proportion on the road's gritty surface. Blood trickled from the ends of her fingers to form dark spots on the road and was washed from her dangling hair by the sweeping rain.

For several long minutes Mor just stood there cradling his daughter in his arms and staring glassy-eyed into her shattered face. Instinctively, he willed her to move. The flicker of an eyelid would have been enough. Just a sign to show that life had not deserted her.

Of course, she did not move. She couldn't. She was dead and he was alone.

Alone.

For the first time he realized that the future was a hell in itself. First his wife, and now Anna. Dear Anna. No longer there to make his supper and keep him company. To fill the house with joy and hope and laughter. To pull him out of those deep, dark depths of despair. The house would now be empty but for the shell of himself. He wouldn't live there anymore. He'd merely exist, hoping every day that he'd be struck down by an incurable disease or a failed heart.

He jerked his head up suddenly and shouted at the sky. “Oh, God, why did you let them do it? Why? Why? Why?”

He dropped to his knees and laid Anna in the road, taking great care to keep her covered with his coat.

Four lights went on in answer to his grief-stricken cry and heads appeared at the windows. Mor stood up and raised his arms in a beckoning gesture. “Anna has been murdered,” he shouted. “My daughter, Anna, has been murdered. For God's sake, come down.”

They appeared in dribbles. Women in belted dressing gowns and indoor slippers and men in overcoats over pyjamas. They approached Mor slowly, horrified by the sight of the bundle on the ground before him. Anna's feet were poking out from under the coat and her hair lay like a mop-end on the road.

An elderly woman in curlers stepped forward, prompted by her husband, and said, “Are you all right, Ross?”

He stared at her unseeingly. “It's Anna,” he said. “She…She's dead. They killed her.”

The old woman turned to her white-faced husband, who knelt stiffly beside the body and gently lifted the coat from Anna's face. He dropped it back in place quickly and struggled to his feet, shaking uncontrollably. “Oh, Ross — who did this terrible thing?”

More people were emerging from their homes. Gradually they ventured nearer to Mor and soon

,

formed a circle round him that was five deep. Shocked faces stared from Mor to his daughter. These were people who knew death only as the inevitable conclusion to old age. Murder and all other crimes of violence were unknown on the island.

A man stepped out of the encircling crowd and peered at Anna under the coat. He was tall and big-shouldered in a heavy ankle-length overcoat and cloth cap. He straightened himself, paused for a moment, and stood facing Ross Mor, who had lowered his head and was sobbing loudly on to his chest. The man reached out and took Mor's shoulders in a firm grip. It showed in his face that he himself was having to fight back the tears.

"Ross," he said gently. "Can you tell me what happened?"

Mor lifted his head, opened his eyes. His face quivered in anguish.

"Angus?" he said.

"Aye, laddie, it's me. Now will you try to control yourself and tell me who is responsible for this?"

Mor closed his eyes to squeeze out the tears and myriad new lines appeared in his forehead.

He said, "Two men . . . wearing masks ... They . . . came to my house and stole the treasure. They had guns."

Angus said, "The treasure! My God."

"When I came down here to raise the alarm I found her."

"Where was she, Ross?" he said.

"The exchange," Mor said with difficulty,

remembering how he had found her lying there in the heather. “She was outside. She must have disturbed them as they were breaking up the equipment. They destroyed the phone lines.”

Angus Campbell's veneer of calmness began to crack and his eyes exploded. “Are you telling me they've cut us off from the mainland? We canna use the phones?”

“That's what I'm saying.”

Angus looked around at the others and saw that they were equally alarmed. Then he returned his attention to his friend. “Where are they now, Ross?”

“I don't know,” Mor said. “They must have a boat somewhere.”

“Then we've got to stop them.”

Mor nodded. “Aye, and we have to kill them, Angus. We've got to kill them for what they have done to Anna.”

Angus nodded understandingly. “They'll get what's coming to them. You can be sure of that.” He glanced quickly at Anna's body and in a gentler voice, said, “You can take Anna to my house, Ross. My wife will watch over her.”

Mor nodded absently but made no attempt to lift his daughter. He just stood there, staring at the ground, as if lost somewhere deep within himself.

Angus turned sharply and addressed the crowd in a loud, savage voice that sounded strangely alien even to his own ears.

“Well, you can all see what these men have done to Anna. I say we go after them. Now.”

The crowd was slow to react. At first they were not quite sure what Angus meant by 'go after them'.

But when it did finally sink in there came cries of "let's get them" and "the bastards deserve to die."

Angus brought order by raising his arms. "Then get dressed quickly and meet me down at the harbour. We'll check on all the possible landing places like the beach and the old jetty and we'll round up those outside the village."

He stood very still for a moment, thinking, then said, "You'll need weapons. Anything you can lay your hands on. Some of you have rifles and shotguns. Bring those. You others can find something. Pitch-forks or knives. We need to call Erchy McGregor and Donald Ruaug. And there's Andrew Maclean. He's staying with Bella McLeod. We'll get him to help as well."

A woman's hysterical cry rose above the heated chatter of the crowd. "Should we no inform the police on the mainland? They'll stop these men."

"How can we, woman?" Angus barked. "We're without phones. And even if we could get through, surely it would be unwise for all our sakes if the police were to learn about the treasure? Are you forgetting that?" He turned to look at Mor, a sympathetic expression touching his mouth. "Besides, if the police were to catch these killers they would only receive a measly prison sentence for what they have done. We ourselves have got to see that they are justly punished."

The small crowd began to disperse, disappearing briefly into their homes and emerging shortly after fully dressed and armed with all manner of weapons.

,

Mor lifted Anna gently in his arms and carried her into the warmth of Angus Campbell's small semi-detached cottage, where he laid her out on the bed upstairs. Angus's portly wife took it upon herself to look after Anna but was unable to persuade Mor to have his injured head seen to.

Within twenty minutes a milling crowd had gathered on the pier. The rain had abated but the wind was still an unremitting force screaming around them.

They were confused, waiting for someone to tell them what to do. This was all so totally strange to them. Not only the terrible business of the murder, but also their own violent intentions.

It was Angus who took the lead.

"First, we'll find out where they left from," he said. "Then we'll set off after them."

One of the boat owners realized suddenly that someone had been tampering with his engine. His loud bellowing cry was carried along the pier. The other two boat owners made the same grim discovery shortly afterwards. They informed Angus that vital parts were missing from all three engines that could not be replaced immediately.

There was uproar.

The shouting and cursing brought Ross Mor out of himself and when he realized what all the commotion was about he called out, "We've got to get them. They can't get away with it. They can't."

The desire to avenge his daughter's death was burning like a fire inside him.

Just then everybody's attention was drawn to a pair of bright headlights approaching the pier from

,

the village. Eventually the crowd could see it was a van. When it came to a stop beneath a street lamp at the head of the pier they saw there were figures inside. The crowd fell silent, curious as to why no one had got out.

Frowning, Mor began to walk towards the van. And that's when the doors flew open and three masked men stepped from it. A fourth remained behind the wheel, his features lost in the gloom beyond the windscreen. Each of the three men was armed with a shotgun.

The one who spoke had a broad London accent. He was looking at Mor, who continued to walk forward fearlessly.

"Don't be a bloody hero, mate," the man warned. "I'm prepared to use this and so help me I will if you come any closer."

Mor stopped. He had no wish to die before he'd made these bastards pay for what they had done.

*

Parker held his shotgun in a firm grip and said, "We want to leave this island without any fuss. So if you don't make trouble nobody will get hurt. Is that clear?"

"You killed her," the man cried out. "You murdered her like she was some animal."

Parker swallowed a huge lump and when next he spoke his voice was high, strained.

"Who the fuck are you?" he yelled.

,

"I'm Ross Mor," the man said. "Anna's father. Why did you have to kill her?"

"I don't know what the frigging hell you're talking about," Parker shouted back. "I admit we came here to take the treasure from you, but that's all. We've killed no one. We're prepared now to hand it back if you'll give us an outboard engine for one of the boats down there."

Mor bared his teeth in a mirthless grin.

"If you didn't kill her, then who did?"

"I've told you — I don't know what you're talking about. Now, do we get to leave this damn island peaceably or are people going to get hurt?"

As if on cue, Ross Mor charged forward, casting all caution aside. He had about fifteen yards to cover before reaching Parker and two shots were fired over his head as a warning. But Mor ignored the threat. He was like a prize bull that has smelled fear in a matador.

Parker could see that Mor was not armed, so he didn't bother to blast him as he ran, and he told the others not to shoot, either. Instead, he waited until Mor was almost on top of him and then smashed the mad Hebridean in the face with the butt of his shotgun.

Mor might have looked like a bull and he might have possessed a bull's strength, but all the same he collapsed to the ground like a knocked-over skittle, blood streaming from one corner of his mouth where a tooth was buried in his lower lip. He was unconscious, but alive.

,

Parker looked up at the men along the pier and tried to anticipate their next move, which was impossible.

There were about twenty of them and most were not a day under sixty. Even so they all seemed pretty fit and formidable. Plus they were all armed.

Hodge, sensing the need for a further display of dominance, raised his gun and fired yet another warning shot at the sky.

He shouted along the pier. “If someone doesn't come up with a fucking engine right now, at this very minute, I'm going to blast your friend here to pieces.”

He lowered the barrel of his gun until it pointed at Mor's head. His hands were dead steady and his expression rock hard.

For some seconds the islanders discussed the situation among themselves, speaking in loud Gaelic voices. Then a tall man in a long dark overcoat snatched a shotgun from one of the others and stepped to the front of the mob. Even from a distance of about twenty yards Parker and the others could see that his hands were shaking.

He spoke with authority, addressing his words to Hodge. “My name is Angus Campbell. I'm a friend of the man you're threatening to kill.” He paused to swallow and to wipe a sweaty palm on his coat. “Let me tell you now that not one of you will leave this island alive if you harm him. So I suggest you put down your weapons and give yourselves up. We far outnumber you and there's nowhere you can run.”

,

"We want a boat," Hodge called out. "And if you want your friend here to live you better go find us one."

Angus yelled back. "I gather from what you say that your own boat is either lost or damaged. Which is indeed unfortunate for you."

At which point, Hodge pulled the trigger.

Ross Mor's head exploded a bloody mess of shattered brain and fragmented skull, leaving nothing above the shoulders. Pieces of charred flesh and bone splashed everywhere and clumps of hair fluttered to the ground like strange, winged insects.

There were bits of him everywhere, for yards around.

The islanders did not move and neither did Parker. He, like them, could only stare in stunned silence at the heap of meat that was once a man.

Hodge, on the other hand, appeared unmoved by what he had done and he seemed unaware of the stinging tension that now filled the air.

Slowly, he raised his gun and called out, "Now, who the hell else wants it?"

It was at that moment the islanders surged forward in an angry mob.

For a brief moment, Hodge stood frozen to the spot, staring wide-eyed at the approaching figures, wondering why his little display of ruthlessness had failed to work. Then suddenly he became aware of the engine revving behind him, and he was wrenched out of his trance-like state.

Turning, he saw Parker clambering to get into the front passenger seat. He ran desperately after the van, which was speeding in reverse without him. He managed to get a tentative grip on the handle and was flung on his back when Maclean applied the brakes to spin the machine around.

He got up quickly, saw the rear doors swing open, and threw himself at them, landing half in and half out of the van. He heard the screech of tyres, the report of a shot, and managed somehow in all the confusion to get on to the back of the van. He snatched a glance back and caught a glimpse of Stewart some yards away. He had fallen over and was screaming something about his foot being hurt.

Hodge realized immediately what had happened. Stewart had been standing against the nearside wing of the van when the crowd began its charge and when Maclean reversed the wheel must have run over his foot, crushing the bones.

Now the angry mob was bearing down on the befallen Scot and there was nothing the others could do to save him. "For pity's sake get moving," Hodge screamed. "He's had it."

Maclean slammed his foot down and the van screeched forward up the slope towards the main street.

FOURTEEN

Angus Campbell stood staring down at the man left behind. The villain had removed his stocking mask and Angus thought what a pathetic looking individual had been hiding beneath it. His eyes stared ahead into nothing and he somehow seemed resigned to the fact that he was going to die a horrible death. His face was a mask of terror, his eyes huge and his skin taut.

A voice behind Angus sounded. "Kill the bastard," and the words were copied by the others who turned it into a chilling chant.

By now these normally placid men had been worked up into a frenzy by the course of events. They hungered for revenge.

"Kill him"

"Murdering bastard."

"Kill him."

An old man of about sixty-five took the initiative. He leapt forward, and the knife in his hand slashed across the villain's forehead, leaving a thin line of blood. The stranger rolled on his side and suddenly the others closed in. They began to kick him and stab him.

"That one is for Anna," one man yelled.

"And that one is for Ross," said another.

The kicking and stabbing continued. In the face, the ribs, the legs. Everywhere. They spat on him, huge dollops of phlegm dripping from his face.

,

Angus wanted to be the one to finish him off. He decided the shotgun he was carrying would be too quick, too merciful. He threw it to the ground and grabbed a pitch-fork from the man standing next to him. The others cheered him on, urging him to kill the snake. Chanting, shouting, kicking.

"Killer."

"Bastard."

"Murderer."

Angus, his eyes fierce with hate, took the fork's handle in a firm two-handed grip and raised it above his head. Then he forced it down with all his strength and the stranger opened his eyes just as the two middle prongs of the fork punctured his throat.

*

Angus stepped back from the body, leaving the fork embedded in the bloody mess that was the man's throat. The handle dropped when he let go, causing the prong-end to flick up and wrench the dead man's chin on to his chest. He looked like he was trying to stare at his own feet over his mound of gut.

Two of the group turned away in horror, one old timer vomited all over himself, and three of them actually smiled. Angus stood there with a blank expression. He did not feel guilty. The villain had deserved it, he reasoned with himself. After all, he was no better than a savage beast. A ruthless killer. He deserved to die like a rat.

,

Lechy, one of Angus's two sons, tapped him on the shoulder. “Are you all right, father?” he said.

Angus turned to him and nodded.

“Aye, laddie, I'm fine.”

“So what do we do now?” the boy asked.

Angus turned from his son to the faces of the men around him. Faces glowing with a new awareness, but still showing signs of having been through a shattering experience.

He said slowly, “There are three more that deserve to die. And I say we show them no mercy. Do you all agree?”

A cheer went up and as Angus turned and walked towards the main street the crowd followed.

FIFTEEN

When they left the village, Maclean turned on to the road which took them up the hill past the battered telephone exchange. Just beyond Ross Mor's place the road descended towards a long beach, revealed by a lacework of phosphorescence. Then it swung inland again to skirt a wind-ruffled lochan.

"Where the hell are we going?" Hodge said from the back.

They were the first words spoken since the mad dash from the pier and they brought home to all three the awful truth of their predicament. The fact was there was nowhere to go except around in circles.

Parker turned slowly in his seat to face Hodge. His expression was cold, hostile.

"That crazy stunt you pulled back there has fucked us," he accused through tight lips.

Hodge merely shrugged. "I thought it would scare them."

"Well, it didn't work, did it? And you can take it from me, you slimy rat, that if these island people don't get you, then I will. You're more dangerous than bloody cancer."

Hodge crawled across the floor, placed his back against the side of the van, and laughed, an obscene, braying sound. His teeth were almost as bright as his eyes in the gloom.

They drove on another half mile in silence and then Maclean braked and switched off the engine. Immediately the wind began to kick the side of the van as it swept around the hill on their right. They were surrounded again by moorland. Bleak and desolate stretches of treeless terrain dissected by a run-down network of dykes. Cotton grass swayed mournfully at the edges of the road and holes in the cloud threw down weird shadows that danced around them like ghosts playing hide and seek.

Maclean tapped his fingers nervously on the wheel and bit into his bottom lip.

“This is ridiculous,” he said. “We can't go on driving around forever.”

“As I see it, we have no choice,” Parker said, matter-of-factly.

So they thought about it. A minute. Two minutes. But it got them nowhere. They were marooned on an island being hunted by a bunch of wild men and their only avenue of escape lay across miles of treacherous sea.

“Look, there’s a chance Bella can help us,” Maclean said. “She knows the island like the back of her hand. I need to go to her. She doesn’t live in the village so she won’t know yet what’s happened.”

“Then let’s go there,” Hodge said. “Find out what the fuck she can do.”

Maclean’s eyes grew hooded. “I’ll go alone,” he said. “I don’t trust you to keep your cool.”

“Bollocks to that,” Hodge fumed.

But Maclean stood firm. “I know a place where you two can hold up. Soon as I sort something I’ll come and fetch you.”

Hodge shook his head. “Forget it. We stick together.”

“Not on your life,” Maclean said. “You’re hyped up and dangerous. I’m not taking a chance that you’ll do something stupid. I’ll handle it. You just have to fucking trust me.”

Hodge backed down and expelled a breath. “So where’s this place you know?”

“It’s an old derelict house up there on the hill,” he said. “It's as good a spot as any and better than most. I’m pretty sure you’ll be safe there, at least for a while. You'll have a bird's eye view of the surroundings in daylight.”

“Does this road go up there?”

“No. This only goes around the island. A circular route. You have to walk if you want to go inland.”

“So how can we find the house from here?” Parker asked.

Maclean pointed. “There's an old dry-stone wall over there to the left a little. Follow that up the hill and it takes you right to the house.”

Hodge leaned forward, frowning. “What about the treasure? We might as well hang on to it as long as we can. We might still be able to take it with us.”

Maclean nodded. “You're right.” He glanced out the window again. “Let’s hide it in the ditch over there.” The ditch ran parallel to the road and long failing grass reared up from its gloomy depths. “We all know where it is so if we can come back for it we will.”

,

With a sense of urgency, they clambered out of the van and unloaded the cases and crates.

"Get back to us as soon as you can," Parker said to Maclean.

"I will," Maclean promised.

As the van moved off, Parker and Hodge started walking up the hill in the dark.

SIXTEEN

Bella's house was on the other side of the island from the village. It was a single-storey brick affair and had been converted from a traditional crofter's cottage.

Maclean drove halfway there in the van before dumping it on the moor. He walked the rest of the way — about a mile and a half—across smelly peat bogs and fields made rough by tufts of grass. He was beginning to feel the cold himself now. That damn perpetual wind he remembered from his childhood had still not ceased.

He cupped his bare hands and blew warm air into his palms. Then he zipped his anorak all the way up to his chin and as he walked on he began to wonder detachedly what had happened to Stewart.

Had he been killed or taken hostage? If he was still alive would he talk and identify his accomplices? Maclean still could not fully grasp what had happened. What a fucking mess.

First that stupid prick Hodge had beaten the girl to death. Then the frigging wind had smashed up the boat. Followed by another bout of madness from The Cowboy.

Jesus.

It was meant to be a doddle. A raid that even a bunch of amateurs could have pulled off. But

,

instead it had all gone horribly wrong and God only knew how it was going to play out.

He halted fifty yards from the croft and climbed onto a low wall. The lights were on in the house and he knew that Bella would be waiting for him. He had told her they would pick her up on their way back to the boat with the treasure. And he had assured her that nothing could go wrong and nobody would get hurt.

He thought about Hodge again, and immediately wished it had been that bastard who'd been left behind on the pier instead of Stewart. Hodge was a crazy man. A bloody psycho, and he, Maclean, should have known better than to have recruited him for the blag.

He pushed from his mind thoughts about what had happened and why it had happened and jumped down off the wall. He had a job to do and there wasn't much time left in which to do it. He guessed that someone would shortly be arriving with news from the village.

He trudged across the next field, plodded through a potato patch and across the back-yard.

Bella heard him enter the kitchen and appeared from the bedroom. She was wearing a coat and shoes and there was a suitcase on the floor next to her. As soon as she saw his face she realized that something was wrong. Her facial muscles tightened

Without preamble, he said, “Things didn’t work out. We have the treasure but some people have been killed.”

Her hand flew to her mouth. “Oh, my God!”

,

He crossed the room and took hold of her hands. They were cold and trembling.

"I wasn't to blame," he said in a shaky voice. "It was one of the others. It was a fucking mess. And to top it all we've lost the boat. It came away from the jetty and was smashed up on the rocks."

Before he was through telling her the whole story she was crying her heart out, her body racked with sobs. He pulled her to him, held her tight and felt a sense of shame so deep it made him sweat.

"This is awful," Bella said through a cascade of tears. "Anna was a friend. And her father was a good man. They didn't deserve to die. My God I can't believe it."

"Neither can I," Maclean said. "And I saw it with my own fucking eyes."

Bella managed to stop crying after about a minute. She took out a hanky and wiped away the tears. Her eyes were red and swollen. She pushed out her lower lip and said, "Where are the others?"

Maclean passed a hand over his face, pressed his own eyes shut. "They're hiding out in a derelict house. They want me to find a way off the island. And to do that I need your help."

She swallowed hard and wiped an arm across her mouth. "What can I do?"

"We need a boat. Any boat. So long as it's got an engine or an outboard. So think carefully. Where can we lay our hands on something?"

At that moment, Bella's face was struck by the lights of a vehicle showing through the window. It had turned on to the track leading to the front of the house.

“Now, keep calm,” Maclean told her. “Take off your coat and hide the case. Tell them I’ve been with you here all evening. They can’t know that I was involved. I’m pretty sure they didn’t see me in the van.”

“But what if the man who was left behind has told them?”

“Then I’m fucked. So we just have to hope he hasn’t.”

“But…”

“Look, you can’t let me down, Bella. My life depends on it. And for that matter so does yours.”

,

SEVENTEEN

Robert McNeil and Johnny Thompson were at the door when Bella answered it. They were both in their late fifties and they looked scared. Bella let them in and they did not seem surprised to see Maclean sitting in an armchair.

"We need you, Andrew," Thompson said. "Something has happened."

Maclean hauled himself to his feet. He had already removed his coat and shoes and wiped the sweat from his face with a towel.

"What is it?" he said.

There followed a verbal encounter between the two islanders as to who could tell the story quickest. Maclean tried not to flinch when they revealed Stewart's fate. He had been stabbed and beaten and finally killed with a pitchfork. In truth Maclean was relieved. At least Stewart hadn't talked.

"We've got to find those bastards, Andrew," Thompson said. "Can we count on your help?"

"Of course," Maclean said. "I'll get dressed. Wait outside and I'll get myself sorted."

"Okay

"We have weapons in the car," Thompson said. "We're getting together in the village to work out a plan of action."

The two men went back outside. As soon as they were gone Maclean took Bella in his arms. She was shaking again and her sallow face felt cold against his.

"You were terrific," he said. "But you have to stay strong, and calm. If I don't go with them they'll get suspicious."

"But what if something happens to you?"

"It won't. I'll come back as soon as I can. Meanwhile, get ready to leave the island. I'll find a way off. I promise."

She looked up at him, her eyes searching his face.

"You must be careful, Andrew. Don't underestimate the men of Stack. They're stubborn and resourceful. They're also unforgiving."

"I know how to look after myself," he said, forcing a half-hearted smile. "Try not to worry."

She shook her head. "How can I not worry? This is a disaster. You said nobody would get hurt. You said it would be easy."

"I know what I said, Bella, and I'm truly sorry for what's happened. But I'll make it up to you. I promise you that."

He gave her a long, lingering kiss on the mouth and put his coat and shoes back on. The two men were waiting for him outside next to a battered VW. He climbed in the back and they drove Maclean to the pier. On the way they described in more detail what had happened to Stewart. He couldn't help thinking that he was a whisker away from meeting the same gruesome fate himself. He said nothing, just prayed that by some miracle a means of escape would present itself.

They went to the village hall. Inside, all the menfolk had gathered, at least forty of them, mostly old men. They each carried a weapon of some kind.

,

Angus Campbell came bounding over, shotgun cradled at his hip. “Andrew,” he said. “Have you been told what’s happened?”

Maclean nodded. “Who are they?” he asked.

Angus shook his head. “We don’t know. But they came here for the treasure.”

Maclean gestured towards the gun Angus was carrying. “What are you planning to do with that?” he said.

“Exact revenge, of course. These men are killers. We have to stop them before they claim more lives.”

“What about the cops?”

Angus shook his head. “We don’t need the police. We’ll handle this ourselves in our own way and deal with the consequences afterwards.”

Maclean cleared his throat. “Then count me in,” he said. “I’m with you all the way. But how did they find out about the treasure?”

Angus narrowed his eyes. “I wondered if you might have let word slip yourself, laddie.”

Maclean tried to appear shocked. “I can assure you I didn't give the name of the island to anyone.”

“What about your dealer friends?”

“I lied to them. I told them the treasure was from a wreck off the Shetlands.”

Angus studied him carefully for a long moment and then shrugged. “It’s something we’ll worry about after we find them.”

“So where are they?”

“We don’t know. But it won't take us long to sniff them out. They're strangers here and they know nothing about the island.”

,

Angus went to the front of the hall where he stood on the platform next to the pulpit. He raised his shotgun to bring order to the gathering and placed the butt-end on the floor.

"We need to coordinate the search," he said. "But we should hold off until dawn. Hunting them down in the dark will be too dangerous. Meanwhile everyone on the island has to be alerted. We need to make sure they're all safe."

There was a brief discussion before everyone started to file out.

As Angus was leaving he said to Maclean, "You come with me, Andrew. We'll visit homes on the north side of the island. Most of those people won't know what's happened yet."

Maclean felt his heart sink. He followed Angus outside.

"You need a weapon," Angus told him. "I have a spare rifle. Will you know how to use it?"

"I'm sure it won't be that hard to learn," Maclean said.

EIGHTEEN

In the morning there was a mist. At first, in the dawn light, it was eerily translucent, creeping over the shadowy landscape like a clear, sticky fluid, consuming everything in its path.

Its density increased along with its size as the morning wore on and very soon the whole island was wrapped in a damp, yellowish blanket. It stirred only gently, indeed almost imperceptibly, in the absence of any wind. A great quietness prevailed, disturbed only by the distant cry of a gull and the amplified activities of insects in the tall, still grass.

The two men sat amongst the depressing ruins of the old Hebridean 'black house', their ears extra-sensitive to the slightest sound, their bodies cold and weary from their long ordeal. Their breathing stirred the greyness around them and their voices — on the few occasions they spoke — seemed unnaturally loud.

The six-foot thick walls, made from large boulders and with rounded corners, stared down at them mockingly through the swirling mist. They were inside the shell of what would once have been the home of a large, hard-working crofting family. But the walls no longer echoed to the sounds of laughter or of children. Now they were merely a

,

refuge for a multitude of climbing weeds and industrious insects.

Naturally, the roof was gone, the thatching having been blown into oblivion over the years, and the inner sanctums of the place were laid naked to the sky.

The two men were sitting with their backs against the wall opposite the narrow opening that had been the door through which generations of a family had passed. Just above their heads was the small shapeless hole that had been the only window. The room itself was about eighteen feet long by fifteen feet wide with a side door leading into the adjoining byre.

Throughout the long night, and despite the cold which had early on worked its way inside his clothing, Parker had been conscious of an almost palpable air of foreboding about the place. It seemed almost as if the old house resented their very presence there. He hadn't let it play on his mind, though, as there were more pressing problems bearing down on him.

Maclean hadn’t yet returned and he knew that time was running out. He suspected that the islanders had decided to wait for daylight before mounting a full search. And when that did get under way it would not take them long to locate the hideout.

They had little choice but to sit and wait and pray that Maclean wouldn’t let them down.

Neither Parker nor Hodge had slept. Both sat with their backs to the wall and their knees tucked

,

up in front of them. The silence between them had been a strained one, taut with tension.

The arrival of the mist had been welcome. Maybe it would make things difficult for the hunters for one thing and give Maclean an opportunity to find a way out.

,

NINETEEN

It was 9.30 a.m by Parker's watch when the first sounds reached them.

He heard a sharp cry over to the left and then two shouts came from the right, seemingly in answer to the first. Were there three of them? Or just two? He couldn't be sure. But they were working their way up the hill towards the ruins for certain and at a guess they were about a hundred yards away.

Another shout. This time from the right and nearer. Sixty yards? Not much further.

"They're spread out," Hodge whispered.

Parker nodded agreement. "They'll be here in a few minutes. Got any bright ideas?"

Hodge caressed the shiny, black barrel of the shotgun.

"If they show their faces here, I know what I'll do."

"Don't be an idiot. You'll bring the lot of 'em up here. We've got to get away from here. Not play at Custer's last stand."

"What about Mac? If we go he won't find us."

"Well, if you want to stay that's your business. I'm going up to the top to look for a way down the other side."

"Okay," Hodge said, "I'm with you."

Parker went back inside to pick up his shotgun. He paused for a moment in the middle of the roofless room and sniffed a couple of times.

"What is it?" Hodge enquired impatiently.

,

"Bloody fag smoke. The place reeks of it."

"So what?"

"Well, for one thing, they'll realize we've only just left and for another they'll know which way we've gone."

"Well, there's nothing you can do about it now unless you happen to have an air freshener handy?"

Outside they heard the voices again, clearer now, and Parker thought he saw a shadow move in the mist just below where they were standing. Instinctively, he tugged at Hodge's arm.

"This way."

They moved quickly but carefully so as not to make a sound. They went round the back of the house to the remains of a well, then started to climb the hill.

The terrain underfoot was predominantly grass, pimpled with bare rock made slippery by the heavy dampness in the mist.

With Parker out in front, the two men scrambled feverishly up the hill, not bothering to look back because visibility was only about thirty feet all round. Their breathing came hard and heavy and very soon they were panting like mad dogs.

It had been years, Parker reflected, since he had run further than the bus stop near his flat — and that was downhill all the way. He just wasn't up to this sort of thing anymore.

They'd gone only a short way when they heard the shot. It was close. Too close. Probably a signal to announce the fact that the group climbing the hill had found something. The derelict house? The cigarette smoke?

,

Parker tried to work out his next move but couldn't. He was paralysed suddenly by the terrible and overwhelming thought that death was inevitable. He couldn't see that there was any way out.

He vaulted on to the nearest flat-topped rock and from there to the next rock up, knowing that Hodge was close behind him. He laboured over stretches of long, wet grass, arms flailing in front of him, legs on the brink of collapsing under the weight of built-up tension and sheer bloody exhaustion.

The mist cleared a path for them as it was stirred into a breeze by the swiftness of their flight. Parker could see only so far ahead and every obstacle reared up at him suddenly out of the mist. A large overhanging rock which had to be climbed using both hands and feet and another that was so slippery he fell on his back when he stepped on to it.

The shouting behind them grew louder and became incessant as those in pursuit sensed how close they were to their prey. Others were being summoned and directions called out as the chase gained momentum. They were preparing to close in, gathering their forces for the final kill.

Parker urged himself on despite the pain in his calves and behind his ribs. His face was dripping sweat and he was beginning to experience a strange light-headedness as his strength seeped out through his open pores. He wasn't sure how long he could maintain his present pace. The hill was so steep. It tore the life from him with every agonising step. The rocks were like wet ice and the grass a soft springy mattress that pulled possessively at his feet.

,

Then, suddenly, they reached the crest.

Parker stopped and Hodge very nearly ran into him from behind. They both stood gasping for breath, trying unsuccessfully to see into the mist through squinting eyes. All was quiet for the moment, but Parker did not allow himself to be lulled into a false sense of security. They were not clear yet. Far from it.

"Here they come," Hodge said.

Parker looked down the hill in the direction they had come. Three ghost-like figures were emerging from the mist. Dark incongruous shapes that appeared almost to be forming before their very eyes. They were approaching slowly, sinisterly, like white hunters stalking a pair of wounded lions.

It was impossible to identify the weapons they were carrying, but it was clear they each held something and Hodge was taking no chances. He raised his gun and fired down the hill. The blast shattered the foggy silence and Parker felt sure the noise would carry all the way across the stretch of sea to Mull.

They weren't able to tell if he'd scored a hit because the figures melted into the mist and they were not going to wait around to see how many of them emerged again.

With Parker once again in the lead, they took off. The ground on top of the hill was less of an assault course, but at the same time it didn't go very far and within seconds it was falling away beneath them and they were unintentionally picking up speed as momentum carried them down the other side.

Parker stumbled once on a rock and rolled painfully across its jagged surface before dropping on to a patch of spongy grass. Hodge helped him to his feet and they were off again, weaving and jumping and colliding with one another in a desperate bid to increase the distance between themselves and their pursuers.

They were halfway down the hill when sunlight suddenly drowned them, its powerful rays striking them like some unseen force and stopping them dead in their tracks.

They had broken out of the mist and looking back it became terrifyingly clear that only the top half of the hill was ringed in a grey, sombre cloak. Remnants of the mist still hung lazily in the air above the stark, undulating landscape below them, but the bulk of it had dissipated during the morning and the green fields and web of dry-stone walls could be seen stretching for about a mile before plunging into the sea. It was a fine day, as before, and the air was clear.

"Down there! Look!"

Parker followed Hodge's stricken gaze and saw a group of five men about half a mile away. They'd stopped whatever they were doing and were pointing up the hill.

"They've seen us!"

The men were over to the left in a field. To the right of them the only sign of life were a few grazing cows. In the distance was a long, sandy beach, and running down to it a narrow, zigzagging stream.

,

“We'll go that way,” Parker said, knowing only too well that if others were rounding the hill from that side, then they'd had it.

TWENTY

Angus Campbell was on the other side of the island above the old jetty when he heard the shot. Three others were with him, including Andrew Maclean. They had been looking down on the remains of the cruiser which had brought the villains to the island.

Most of the debris was scattered over the chaos of rocks on either side of them, but some parts were still sloshing about on the water and thudding against the jetty timbers. Evidently the boat had taken a severe battering from the rocks just offshore and although the main body of it had gone down, a good deal of it had been torn off and had subsequently found its way to the surface.

The shot came like a sting in the heart for Maclean. He had been listening for it all morning, anticipating the worst. He hadn't thought it would take them long to find the other two once the mist cleared lower down. And there was nothing he could do about it. He felt impotent and frustrated. Somehow he had to break away from the mob and find a way off the island.

"They've spotted them!" Angus cried out.

A second later, Maclean was chasing the others across a field. Angus was out in front, looking like a mercenary soldier leading a bunch of maniac followers to a massacre. But there was at the same time an air of absurdity about the charging group,

,

particularly as the eldest one, a man in his late sixties, was barely managing to stay on his feet as his ageing limbs began to falter with the effort of running.

It took them fifteen minutes to arrive at the bottom of the hill and by that time they needed to stop for a few minutes to catch their breaths.

There was no sign of human activity above them at this point. The hill climbed steeply into the mist which appeared to be thinning gradually. They heard a second shot whilst running and there was no doubt it had come from the hill.

Angus said, “They've probably chased them over the top.”

Maclean was at a loss to know what to do and he felt that he had let Parker and Hodge down.

“Andrew, are you listening to me?”

He hadn't realized Angus had been talking to him. “Sorry. What were you saying?”

“I was telling you and Hamish to follow me. We'll circle the hill to the north. Donald and Lechy will go up and over. Okay?”

Maclean nodded. “Whatever you say.”

He had hoped he might be able to lead them in another direction, away from the gunfire, but he hadn't been given the opportunity to come up with a good enough reason.

Once again he found himself at the rear of a charging group of men.

They plunged through a cold stream, over a low boundary wall and across rough, wet fields. All the way Maclean racked his brain for an idea — a way to prevent Parker and Hodge from becoming trapped in an impregnable net of armed men. But a solution escaped him and there seemed little likelihood that one would occur to him in time. Parker and Hodge had already been spotted and the net was about to drop over them.

Another wall loomed up and since it was higher than the previous ones all three of them halted before it. Angus placed one foot on a jutting boulder and heaved himself up with a loud exhalation of breath. He then reached down and helped the older man up before giving similar assistance to a whacked-out Maclean.

Maclean himself was about ready to collapse. He was that tired. The fact that he was just about managing to keep pace with the others said very little for his own state of health and a great deal more for the island way of life.

When they were all seated on top of the wall, their hearts pounding in unison, Maclean caught sight of two distant figures on the shoulder of the hill ahead of them. They were tearing down the incline, one behind the other, fleeing from the cloud that strangled the top.

Angus saw them too and cried out, "Over there."

Maclean stood up on the wall. There was only one remote farmhouse out there, surrounded by fields. A long strip of lush green machair separated the fields from high rolling sand dunes that dropped on to a pearl-white beach.

Parker and Hodge reached the bottom of the hill and started racing across the first of the fields towards the sea. And then, above them, a group of five men emerged from the mist. Maclean noticed at

,

the same time that there were other figures in the picture. They had just rounded the bottom of the hill from the other side and were obviously the reason why Parker and Hodge were heading for the beach. It meant they were now trapped, hemmed in on all sides, and with little or no chance of escape.

,

TWENTY ONE

They had no choice but to stand and fight. But against how many? Twenty at least. Maybe more. And since they were fast running out of ammunition the odds against them seemed insurmountable.

Parker did not dwell on the whys and wherefores of their perilous predicament as he bolted across the field towards the dunes.

The earth was soft down here in the shadow of the hill and it made progress all the more difficult. Ahead of them and to the right there was an isolated farmhouse. But by Parker's reckoning the group to the right would easily beat them to it if they decided to try for it.

No, they had to make it to the dunes and hope to God they could disappear among the humps of sand that were visible among the low-lying machair.

But for how long they would be able to remain concealed just didn't bear thinking about. Not very long, though, that was for sure. The dunes did not stretch that far along the coast and from up on the hill Parker had observed that they were not very wide.

They came to an old byre, reeking of cows' dung, and Parker paused with his shoulder against it to rest his aching legs. Hodge stopped beside him and turning back they saw the three-pronged attack was advancing quickly.

,

A group of five men were descending the hill and two groups of three were approaching from the left and right. Still about three hundred yards away but gaining ground fast.

And then the sound of a shot, seeming to come a split second before the bullet hit the wall of the byre between them.

They both ducked and scrambled round to the other side of the byre in a panic-stricken rush. So at least one of the bastards had a rifle, Parker thought, which he obviously knew how to use.

Keeping the byre between themselves and the group to the north — from where Hodge believed the shot had come — they broke into another run, this time making a point of keeping their heads down.

The machair was much easier on their feet as the grass was smooth and relatively short. Soon, though, they were over it and on to the sand, which immediately slowed them down.

Wading through the soft flowing whiteness was a nightmare. The men behind were quickly closing the gap and it was only a matter of time before the rifleman had another crack.

They headed for the highest dune, which happened to be the nearest one, and dived into the long grass growing up one side of it. Behind them the sea, a calm, glittering green, was gently stroking the shore and gulls fluttered and squawked overhead.

Parker crawled into a position so he could look back the way they'd come.

The islanders were slowing, obviously hesitant to approach the dunes now that Parker and Hodge were out of sight. The two groups on the flanks were making their way to the centre and Parker assumed they would meet and formulate a plan of action.

He turned to Hodge, lying beside him in the grass and said, “As I see it, we haven't a prayer.”

Hodge rolled on his back and stared at the sky, his chest heaving with every breath. Sweat dribbled from his forehead on to his black tangled hair and from his cheeks on to the sand. A gull flew over him, its shadow caressing his features, and when he turned to Parker his face wore a hollow expression.

“How many guns you reckon they've got?” Hodge asked.

Parker looked towards the islanders who were converging into a single group.

“Impossible to tell from here. We'll have to assume those out there have at least two between them. When the others arrive on the scene, though, they'll probably have a couple more.”

“D'you think they'll come after us, or wait for reinforcements?”

Parker shook his head. “It's my guess they'll come in. They won't take a chance on us sneaking away along the coast while they stand around out there.”

“Well, I hope to God they do just that. Right now I want more than anything to blow a few fucking heads off.”

“Go for whoever's carrying a gun,” Parker advised. “We need all the ammo we can lay our hands on.”

Parker glanced over his shoulder, keeping his head low. The dunes humped their way for about forty yards before dropping on to the beach. On either side of them they stretched about half a mile each way. To the left, the south, the coastline ran up into steep, bird-infested cliffs. The other way, the cliffs were not so high, and the grass on top plunged down almost to touch the sea's slate grey surface.

Parker could guess what they were up to. Two groups were branching out to the left and right of them. They would probably wait at either end of the line of dunes or might even work their way towards the centre, squeezing himself and Hodge in a vice and forcing them to flee from the dunes towards the guns out front.

Parker didn't realize until it was too late that Hodge had taken aim. The blast of the shotgun sent his head spinning and the noise reverberated in his ears.

Ahead of them a group of men scattered and Parker saw immediately a body sprawled in the grass.

“That’s one down,” Hodge said. “Now let’s try to get the fuck out of here.”

TWENTY TWO

But they didn't get very far before they were spotted. The cries of the gulls overhead were drowned suddenly by an acrimonious bellow from the mouth of a thick-set man wearing a reefa jacket and holding, incongruously, a pitch-fork, which stood taller than he did in the sand next to him.

He was standing at the top of one of the dunes, watching like some predatory bird as they slogged through the ankle-deep sand. They were in a hollow between the dunes, south of their previous position, and the going seemed to be getting tougher. The man gave another cry and then started down after them, waving the pitch-fork like it was a flagpole.

Parker and Hodge ran, slowly, clumsily, fighting every inch of the way against the soft, deep sand. The man was some twenty yards behind them, one minute screened by a mound of sand, the next in sight and yelling for them to stop.

They veered to the left, up and over the shoulder of a grass-flecked dune and then into a deep and difficult trench that took them into yet another hollow.

"Just hold it there."

The rasping voice brought them to a sudden halt. It belonged to a short, thin man with a dyspeptic expression who didn't look a day under sixty. He was holding a long, slender hunting rifle in a pair of bony hands. And they had almost run into him. He had popped up from behind a dune and they were only about seven feet from the muzzle of the gun held snugly against his hip, finger poised on the trigger.

Parker felt his shoulders sag and, totally exhausted, he dropped to his knees. Hodge stood motionless, wondering whether he could lift his own gun and drop the man before he was blasted himself. He decided he couldn't. It'd be suicide. But he didn't give up the gun directly when the man gestured for him to do so. Parker did, however, by placing his in the sand next to him.

"Put your gun down," the man said to Hodge. "Or so help me I'll shoot you."

The guy aimed his weapon unsteadily at Hodge's belly, but it was as clear as day that he didn't want to have to use it. He struggled with his conscience, which finally won over, and he raised the barrel skywards and fired a shot that was meant to bring the others running.

Of course it was a mistake. The biggest mistake he had ever made in all his life. Before he'd even lowered his rifle he was reeling backwards from the blast of Hodge's shotgun, his face registering both surprise and pain, his fingers clawing instinctively at the huge gaping hole in his belly as if to try and push back the thick slimy entrails that came gushing forth.

He was dead before he hit the sand and his hands fell to his sides, permitting his insides to rise up through the hole in his body like some horribly misshapen foetus. Hodge stared down at him for a long moment with gloating eyes, then he stepped forward and picked up the rifle. As he turned with it in his hands he saw the pitch-fork carrier back among the dunes, watching them, uncertain as to whether or not he should proceed. Hodge fired from waist level and the bullet pounded into the sand inches from the man's left foot, sending him leaping for cover.

Hurriedly, Parker picked up his own gun and they were off again, leaping over the dead man and wading on through the sand.

But minutes later they were confronted yet again and this time the odds were stacked firmly against them.

Four men.

They came charging out of nowhere into a large, grass-free clearing. Two to the left, two to the right. Two armed with shotguns, one with a lethal-looking scythe and the other a long kitchen knife.

As Parker let loose, the four islanders dived for cover, one of them raising himself quickly to return the fire before both Parker and Hodge had reached the cover of the nearest dune. But the first shot went astray and they were safely screened by the time a second and third shot came their way.

They darted to the left and then saw the fields ahead of them, rolling away towards the hill in the distance. Another shot exploded behind them but they kept running, determined now to break clear of the dunes and try to get out of range of those bloody shotguns.

It was then they saw him.

Maclean.

,

In fact they very nearly ran into him. He was alone, standing on the grass beyond the dunes. He became aware of them at the same time. His gaze was unsteady and from his stupefied expression it was obvious he hadn't been expecting them to appear.

They were just as surprised to see him and even more surprised at the rifle he was holding.

When he saw how they were looking at the rifle he raised it slightly and stepped forward to say something.

But at the same time Hodge lifted his own rifle threateningly.

Parker knew instinctively what Hodge was thinking – that Maclean had changed sides to save his own skin.

So what followed was inevitable.

Maclean moved like lightning, crouching and getting off a shot first. The bullet tore into Hodge's left eye and came out through a fist-sized hole at the back of his head. Then he fired a second time and the bullet rammed into Hodge's chest, knocking him at least two feet into the air.

Parker looked from Hodge to Maclean and the anger rose in him. He heaved his body sideways and squeezed the trigger. Click. Oh, Christ! The ruddy thing's empty!

Behind him, the sound of voices. Excited, loud, hostile. Coming closer.

He lunged forward, lifted the gun by the barrel and swung it at Maclean, catching him on the side of the neck, sending him tripping backwards.

And then Parker was standing over him, looking down, hatred pouring from him, his mouth spewing obscenities.

The shotgun was poised inches above Maclean's forehead and because he was unable to comprehend the strange, almost pleading expression on Maclean's face, he didn't hold back. The butt-end crashed down and Maclean went limp.

Parker didn't stand around to see what damage he'd done. He didn't care, anyway.

He turned to look back, saw five men struggling to get to him through the dunes, and then he fled, out across the field and it wasn't until he was well out of range of their weapons that he realized he hadn't thought to pick up a gun that was loaded.

TWENTY THREE

Parker didn't bother knocking when he came to the little crofter's cottage. He simply pushed open the front door and stomped in. It was empty and he guessed the family had already been evacuated to the village for their own good. They'd left behind greasy plates, which were piled high in the kitchen sink, and on the table there was a half-eaten loaf of crusty bread and a sharp knife.

Four places had been set and he wondered fleetingly if any of the men who had so far been killed was the bread-winner of this particular household. Would the woman who had prepared the meal only hours before return home later as a widow?

He pushed the thought resolutely from his mind as he hurriedly searched the rest of the cottage. It didn't take him long. The rooms were small and there wasn't much in the way of furniture.

Back in the kitchen he found a grubby plastic shoulder bag in one of the cupboards. Into it he stuffed the bread and the knife and a packet of digestive biscuits from on top of the sideboard.

The larder was well stocked, mostly with tinned food, which he left, but a lump of cheese, and a dozen ripe tomatoes he took. There was also a bottle of lemonade and three juicy-looking apples. He took those as well and when the bag was bulging he went to the window and looked out.

He could see them in the distance, coming across the fields away from the dunes and he knew he'd have to hurry if he wanted to get away from there without being seen.

He used the back door this time and found himself in a small yard where a dozen or so chickens were charging around and a load of peats formed a pile six feet high. He climbed over a low wall and, crouching, looked about him.

He estimated the distance between himself and the foot of the next hill at about four hundred yards and he reckoned he could probably make it before they reached the cottage and were able to see beyond it.

But what good would it do him now to gain the high ground without the rifle? No, he'd have to go around the hill, try his luck on the other side of the island where the land wasn't so flat and therefore offered more cover.

More than anything he needed a place to hide out. Somewhere he could rest and think and have time to regain his strength. Later, maybe, when it was dark, he'd try to seek out a means whereby he could leave the island.

He chuckled suddenly, a low, braying sound. Who was he kidding? Certainly not himself. There was no way out now. Deep down he knew it but was afraid to admit it because the moment he accepted the inevitability of the situation, that would be the end of it. The longer he stayed out of their way and the further he ran, the longer he

,

breathed and the more chance there was of a miracle.

He stood and moved off with his head down. Above him the sky was clear and blue, but dark, puffy clouds were moving in from the north, threatening rain. He prayed it would rain, not just a shower, but a heavy, prolonged downpour that would reduce visibility. For he needed all the help he could get now if he intended staying alive.

TWENTY FOUR

When Maclean came to, he was lying on top of a bed and an obese woman with a crinkled face was pawing his aching forehead with a damp cloth. Her breath stank and her large pendulous breasts threatened to crush his chest when she bent over him to inspect the wound at close quarters. He didn't know her name, but he knew her to be the island postwoman and that she doubled as the nurse and midwife.

Fortunately, it wasn't serious, she said. The swelling was the colour of a rotten apple and twice the size, but the skin had not split and there was no blood. It was painful, though, that she could see for herself from the expression on his face when he tried to move his head to look around the room. But he'd live, she assured him, which was more than she could say for those other poor devils.

He asked her what had happened to the man who'd done it and she said he'd got away by outrunning those who were chasing him. But it was known he had come around to this side of the hill and since it was naturally assumed he would head for the wood near the lochan that's where they were going to concentrate the search.

After plumping up his pillows and helping him to sit up straight, she said, "Tis a terrible thing that's going on. I can't see why you don't leave 'em for the police to catch. Already three good men have been killed. Dear God, how many more have got to die

,

before you stupid menfolk come to realize that this is not the right way to go about it?"

He saw tears in her eyes then and one dropped on to her left cheek. She must have felt it because she wiped it away quickly with the back of her hand. Then, as if to save face, she turned away from him and waddled duck-like to the door.

"Bella Macleod is outside asking after yer health," she said, looking back. "D'yer want me say that she can come on in?"

"Yes. I'd like to see her. And thanks."

"Ach, it was nothing."

Bella was relieved to see him sitting up. She rushed across to the bed and buried her head against his chest, weeping softly in slight convulsive shudders. He ran his fingers gently through her hair, enjoying the softness of it.

She looked up at him, red-eyed and beautiful, and said, "It's a sure sign the Lord was with you, Andrew."

He assumed she was referring to the fact that Parker's rifle had been empty when he'd pulled the trigger.

"Then you know what happened?" he said.

"Angus told me. They saw it all as they were running to get to you. He said you shot one of them and the other tried to shoot you but his gun was empty so he hit you instead."

"That's about it."

"Who was the one who got away?" she asked.

He lowered his voice so that if anyone was eaves-dropping outside the door they wouldn't hear him.

,

"His name's Parker," he said, and an image of the man starring down at him malignantly flashed in his mind.

"So why did they try to kill you?"

"It was a mistake of sorts," he said. "They appeared out of nowhere and saw me with the rifle. They didn't give me a chance to explain why I had it and obviously assumed I intended using it on them."

"You mean they thought you were trying to save yourself by going after them?"

He nodded.

"The fools," she said.

He nodded again and shrugged. "Talk about a bloody cock up."

He put his finger under her chin and lifted her head. "Look, Bella, I've got to get away from here before they catch Parker. He might tell them about me. About us."

"But they'll probably kill him before he talks."

"Even so, the ferry will be here tomorrow and an investigation will be mounted. It won't take the police long to sus me out." He stared into her face searchingly for a few seconds. "I want you to come with me, Bella. Tonight."

She spoke without hesitation. "Of course. I said I would. Nothing has changed in that respect."

"That's my girl. Have you had any luck with a boat?"

"Not much, but I've found out that there's an outboard motor in the tackle shed at the harbour. It can be fitted to any of the small craft down there."

“I'll get it after dark then,” he said. “We’ll load as much of the treasure on board as we can. I’ll need another van, though. Can you find one?”

“I’ll try.”

Bella got up suddenly and went across to the window, looking down. Her voice was soft, a whisper. “From now on we'll always be running, won't we? Living in fear of being found out for the rest of our lives.”

The statement surprised him and he groped for the right words. “Not always, love. We'll go far away, use other names. It’ll be all right. You’ll see.”

She turned to face him and the tears were back in her eyes. “I didn't think it would be like this. You said there would be no killing. You promised. And already three men have been murdered. Three men I've known all my life. And then there’s Anna.”

“I know how you feel and I'm sorry. What more can I say? It wasn't my doing. If all had gone to plan we'd be back in England by now.”

“But I feel partly to blame for their deaths.”

“The one person who is to blame is dead himself,” he cut in. “And killing him was the biggest act of charity I've ever done in my life.”

“But that doesn't change what's happened,” she said.

She broke down then in a paroxysm of tears and he forced himself up from the bed and went to her despite the pain that exploded in his head. He put his arms around her and squeezed her, hoping his own strength would pour into her, make her feel more secure and less vulnerable.

,

Voices outside drew his attention to the window and he turned to look out. What he saw caused him to loosen his grip on Bella. He stepped closer to the window for a better view and the scene on the street below brought a lump to his throat.

The bodies of the two dead islanders were being carried into a house opposite and alongside them were two hysterical women. One of them was trying to shake her husband back to life, screaming, crying, stumbling over herself to keep up with the two men bearing the body. The other woman was yelling at the sky, her face pleading, her hands clenched into tight fists.

Maclean shuddered when he realized that he was ultimately responsible for making them widows. This and the events of the past few hours cut deep into his conscience. He felt ashamed of himself. After all, these had once been his people, some were even distantly related to him by blood, and yet his carefully constructed plan had so far succeeded only in bringing misery and disaster into their lives.

At that moment there was a knock at the door and, without waiting for an answer, Angus Campbell came in wearing a lugubrious expression and looking very tired.

He showed no surprise at seeing Bella, for their relationship had always been an open one. He came in and closed the door behind him.

“It's good to see that you're well, Andrew,” he said, his voice low and ragged.

Maclean wondered what the big islander would do to him if he discovered the truth and the thought made his flesh crawl.

“Any news?” Maclean asked, as he pulled away from Bella and returned to the bed.

Angus removed his cloth cap and ran a hand through his hair. He came further into the room and settled in a wooden chair at the foot of the bed.

“Some of the lads are out at the wood now looking for the one who clobbered you” he said. “There's been no sign of the fourth man, yet. We've combed this side of the island thoroughly enough, so we can only assume he's on the other side. We'll get him sooner or later, though, don't you worry.”

“Then you're not going to wait for the police after what's happened?”

Angus raised his arms in exasperation. “Not you as well, laddie. That's all I've been hearing from the womenfolk. Leave it to the law, they say. And meanwhile those murdering thugs roam around out there wrecking and looting our homes. No matter that they might shoot more of us in the process. We just can't stand by and let them get away with it. We've got to stand up for ourselves.”

“What if you still haven't caught them by the time the ferry arrives tomorrow?” Maclean said.

Angus shrugged. “I don't think I'll have much say in the matter then. The women will make sure the authorities are brought into it despite the treasure. They'll want to get on with funeral arrangements and such. But it would be a bloody pity if the law was to take them. They'll no suffer enough is what I'm thinking. They deserve to die a coward's death.”

TWENTY FIVE

Parker couldn't see the wood from the derelict cottage in which he was holed up and therefore didn't know they were concentrating their efforts on it. And since he hadn't seen another human being in almost an hour, he was beginning to wonder if they'd packed it in for the day and gone home.

His hideaway was right out in the open on the moors and clearly visible in daylight to anyone who came within half a mile of it. It was the isolation of the place and the stark nakedness of the moorland around it which had drawn him to it. For it would be impossible for anyone to get close to him during the day without him seeing them. And in the event that they did come he could run in any of a dozen directions.

He was feeling cold now and lonely. He longed for the warmth and comfort of his tiny centrally heated flat in London. How long could he sustain his will to live he didn't know and hated to think. But gradually and inevitably the strength in both his mind and body was being sapped and soon, he feared, he would stop running.

He had been reflecting on what had happened. He and Hodge had given Maclean no chance at all to offer an explanation. Had leapt straight at the obvious conclusion. Mightn't they have been wrong? Done Maclean an unforgivable injustice? He thought back to the incident and recalled that Maclean had been about to say something just as

Hodge had gone for him. Was he going to tell them that they were making a terrible mistake? That he was still on their side, fighting against insurmountable odds to find a way out for them?

No. It was impossible. Crap. Loaded rifle. Running with the mob. It all added up. And even if he hadn't actually intended shooting at them himself, he was doing precious bloody little to stop the others doing so.

But supposing he had been looking out for them. Supposing he'd been hoping they'd emerge from the dunes so he could give them the rifle… No, it couldn't be. He refused to accept it. The facts spoke for themselves, didn't they?

He slept for a couple of hours. He hadn't wanted to, but fatigue swamped him like a thick, black cloud as he sat on the floor with his back propped up against a wall. He dreamt of home, of the comforts he had never really appreciated.

When he woke, a strange pinkish glow permeated the air inside the cottage. Dusk. The sun striving to resist the onslaught of another night.

He wondered if he had seen the sun for the last time. If by morning he'd be dead. The oppressive gloom which coated the landscape outside enhanced his feeling of loneliness. It was as if the whole world had turned against him.

He got to his feet and looked through one of the window apertures. If he waited for a while before moving off it would be pitch dark. He could move about the island with impunity then, go to the very edge of the village without being seen. He had no preconceived plan of action. He'd just have to play it by ear, see what developed.

He waited for an hour, pacing the floor and rubbing his hands together to keep the blood circulating.

It was a clear night. The air still, the stars bright, and no clouds to speak of. If only he could find a boat. the sea would be his friend tonight. He was sure of it.

There was no door to the cottage, just an opening. He pulled up the hood of his anorak and went out into the night. There were no lights showing anywhere and he was thankful there was a full moon. It defined the landscape for him, making shadows from dykes and byres.

He headed the way he'd come, back towards the road. Once there, he'd turn north and walk towards the village. That much he had already worked out in his mind. Maybe he'd come across a remote farmhouse that was occupied. A woman alone, perhaps, who would make the perfect hostage. He doubted that he would be so lucky, though. By now everyone would be in the village, relying on the principle of safety in numbers to keep them out of harm's way.

He trudged across a couple of fields. Without the wind to torment the island the place was disturbingly quiet.

Thick mud clung to the soles of his shoes, making the going that much tougher, and it wasn't long before he was panting and sweating. His breath clouded in the frosty air and his nose felt as if it was about to fall off. The sleep had revived him a little,

,

but it had failed to replenish his store of energy which had been drained completely that afternoon. Having walked only a few hundred yards, he was beginning to feel the strain.

He climbed over a low wall and rested for a few minutes. Whilst sitting there cross-legged on the ground, he longed for a cigarette or a stiff, gut-burning drink, anything to calm his nerves.

Then he was off again, across a field, through a stream, around a lochan and over the shoulder of a hill. He came to the road. He was on an incline there and across the road and beyond it he could see the lights of the village glittering in the darkness. Keeping to the road he turned right and headed towards the lights.

The vehicle, when he saw it, was a hundred yards ahead of him. Its rear lights glowed like the devil's eyes, tiny luminescent blobs of red on black canvas. It appeared to be stationary and occasionally the lights were blotted out by figures moving in front of them.

He left the road and keeping parallel to it he crept down the hill.

He was careful not to make a sound as he approached the vehicle. He got to within about twenty yards, his body merging with the blackness, and from there he was able to see and hear what was going on.

There were two men and a Land Rover. One of the men was kneeling next to the front nearside wheel and Parker gathered from the snips of conversation he was able to pick up that they had a flat tyre. The man kneeling was cursing as he attempted to change it with the aid of a high powered torch nestling on the ground. The other man, visible in silhouette, was standing a couple of feet back smoking a cigarette and holding what looked like a rifle or shotgun.

"Come on, man, hurry up, will ya," said the man with the gun, his voice raised impatiently.

"I'm working as fast as I can," the man kneeling replied. "If you think you can do better then you're welcome to have a go. If not, just shut up and keep an eye out. One of them could be out there right now watching what we're doing."

Crouching low, Parker moved around to the left until he was at the road and the Land Rover was on his right. Then, after first checking to make sure no one was looking his way, he crept across the road, immersing himself in the long grass on the other side.

From there he had no trouble getting up close to the Land Rover and as it turned out he arrived just in time. He heard the clang of metal on the road and then a voice. "At bloody last. Now get that old tyre on the back and let's get going."

He watched and waited, crouching in the grass near the front of the Land Rover. He heard the man with the tyre complaining as he carried it to the rear.

The other man, carrying the gun, came around the front, pausing for a moment to drop the end of his cigarette and tread it into the road. Then he opened the front passenger door and started to get in.

Parker leapt to his feet, took two strides forward, and sent a solid punch into the small of the man's

,

back. The man yelled out and teetered back on his heels. Parker aimed his next blow at his throat which stifled a cry and brought him to his knees. The gun clattered to the ground and Parker managed to get hold of it before the other man came around from the back to see what was going on. When he saw the shotgun in Parker's hands he froze, almost choking on a word that failed to materialise.

"Move and I'll splatter your brains all over the island."

The man instinctively raised his arms. He was middle-aged and clad in duffle coat and gumboots. It was too dark to distinguish his features.

The man on the ground started moaning, so Parker brought the shotgun crashing down on his skull. He fell forward and lay sprawled in the road, face down.

"Now listen," Parker said to his pal. "I want you to get behind that wheel and drive wherever I tell you. You'll do everything I say as soon as I say it. Is that understood? If you so much as speak without being told I'm going to blow you apart. Got that?"

The man nodded.

"Right. Then let's get going. Take me into the village. And remember, I'll be in the rear pointing this thing at the back of your head the whole time."

,

TWENTY SIX

The suitcases and crates were where they'd left them. Maclean lowered himself into the ditch and started lifting them out. It took over ten minutes to load them up onto the back of the old truck he'd picked up in the village.

He covered them with a tarpaulin and got in behind the wheel. He slammed the door shut and glanced at his watch. Seven o'clock. Not bad. He was making good time all things considered.

Next stop was the harbour where he would fit a motor to a boat and stash as much treasure on board as he could manage. Then he'd travel the half mile or so of coastline to where Bella would be waiting on the old jetty. All being well they would then leave the island together and embark on a new life.

He drove slowly, headlights on, into the village and down to the harbour. He passed over the spot where Stewart had been killed. The body had long since been removed. He had no idea what they had done with it.

He noticed the black form of a man outside the tackle shed. He wasn't surprised. He knew someone would be stationed here like a sentry protecting the harbour.

As the man stepped into the beam of the truck's headlights Maclean saw that he was armed with a shotgun. Maclean stopped the truck, switched off the lights and climbed out.

"Oh, it's you, Andrew," the man said, obviously relieved. "You had me worried there for a bit."

Maclean recognised him. He was Jamie Fraser. He was in his twenties and built like an ox.

Maclean glanced back over his shoulder but there was no sign of life behind him. The pier was deserted and the houses with their backs to the harbour had their curtains drawn.

Turning back to Jamie, he said. "Sorry to disturb you like this, Jamie, but there's something I want to ask you."

Jamie's brow creased into a frown and he took another step forward. He didn't even see Maclean's first punch. He only became aware of it when he felt the pain on his chin which tore a screech from his throat.

He staggered back against the double doors of the tackle shed, causing them to rattle on their hinges. The shotgun fell to the ground as he tried to steady himself.

Maclean quickly picked up the shotgun and used it to whack Jamie over the head. The young man grunted as he doubled over. Maclean hit him three more times for good measure and he collapsed in a heap, unconscious and spilling blood profusely from the side of the head.

Maclean wanted to make sure that he wouldn't wake up after just a few minutes. And having administered the beating he was pretty sure that he wouldn't. But he feared he had gone too far. Jamie was very still and might even have stopped breathing. But there was no time to confirm it one way or the other. If he'd added another victim to the

,

body count then he was sorry but there was no time to dwell on it now.

He then turned his attention to the tackle shed. Luckily the double doors were not locked. He opened one side and peered in at the darkness. He saw the distinctive white outline of the small outboard motor just inside the door up against the wall.

But first he had to get Jamie out of sight. He took the young man's hands and dragged him into the shed. Then he quickly covered the body with a pile of damp and heavy fishing nets that he found on the floor. He was about to take charge of the outboard when he heard a noise out front. A vehicle. His heart stopped and he just stood there, not moving or breathing, as the engine note grew louder. It was coming down the road from the village. He was sure of it.

He moved to the door and pulled it to, peering out through the crack.

It was a Land Rover and it had stopped just along the road to his left next to the pier. Its engine was left running and its lights stayed on.

,

TWENTY SEVEN

Parker leant forward and spoke in the driver's ear.

"What's that truck doing over there?"

The man shook his head. "I don't know. I swear it."

Parker looked again at the truck and then at the large wooden shed outside which it was parked.

"What's the shed used for?" he asked.

"It's a tackle shed," the man replied. "Nets and fishing equipment are stored in it."

"The outboard motor you told me about. Is that where it's kept?"

The man glanced nervously at Parker's face in the rear view mirror and nodded.

Parker studied carefully the area around the shed as they closed in on it. He couldn't see any movement and the doors appeared to be shut.

The Land Rover pulled up next to the truck and Parker ordered the driver to hand him the keys. Then he got out before telling the driver to do the same. All was still. Only the water murmured as it rippled around the hulls of the boats tied to their moorings.

Parker told the man to walk in front and they went up to the shed. He gestured for the guy to open the door and go in first. The guy didn't argue.

Inside nothing stirred. The place had a musty smell to it. There were fishing nets strewn across

,

the floor and lobster pots piled high. Parker saw the outboard engine just inside the door. He breathed an audible sigh of relief.

"Is there petrol in it?" he said.

The man nodded. "It's always kept full."

"D'you know how to fit it to a boat?"

"Aye."

"Then let's do it. And for your own sake don't do anything silly this late in the game. With any luck I'll be away from here in a little while and you'll get to see another day."

He watched the man lift the engine and struggle outside with it. He carried it across the road and down the stone steps opposite the tackle shed.

Parker pointed to the largest boat, the only one that looked big enough to get him across the ten miles or so of sea to Mull. It was a skiff with a small covered area that could hardly be called a cabin and a large area of deck space.

When the islander finished attaching the engine Parker nudged him at gunpoint back to the tackle shed. Once inside Parker clobbered him with the rifle butt and the guy went down like a sack of potatoes.

Then Parker turned to go outside.

But he never made it.

Too late, he saw a dark figure spring up at him from behind the pile of lobster pots to his right. Before he could react he felt something solid smash against the back of his head and he was plunged into a deep, dark hole.

TWENTY EIGHT

The coughing of the engine woke him. It must have registered somewhere inside his brain for it encouraged his mind to struggle free from under the blanket which had dropped over it. The pain, when he became conscious, was severe enough to paralyse him for a few seconds and only by a determined effort of willpower was he able to stop himself slipping back into the void.

He groped for a handhold, found it on the side of the lobster pot, and hauled himself to his feet. Then he nearly tripped over the unconscious islander in his efforts to get to the door. But he managed to get one side open and stagger outside in time to see the boat. It was putt-putt-puttering away from him out of the harbour, leaving behind a trail of churned-up water.

He could just make out the figure crouched in the boat alongside what looked like suitcases.

Maclean. It had to be.

And with some of the treasure.

He watched with a sunken heart as the boat was devoured by the night. So Maclean must have been in the shed when they arrived, preparing for his own escape from the island. And the bastard had decided to go it alone rather than risk revealing himself.

Parker's hatred for the Scot became such an emotional force inside him that for a moment it prevented him from dwelling on his own hopeless predicament. That didn't strike home until he was back behind the wheel of the Land Rover.

He turned the ignition key and the engine roared into life. He felt a strange numbness as he engaged gear and pressed his foot down on the accelerator pedal.

He drove hard and fast back through the village and along the road that he knew would take him nowhere. He had no idea what to do or where to go.

He caught a glimpse of his own reflection in the mirror and the strain of the past two days showed on his face. There were new, deep lines around the eyes, which themselves were empty of any kind of expression. His forehead was creased in a permanent frown and his unwashed hair was an indescribable mess. He was a man without hope; lost, scared and trapped.

He saw the girl just in time and had to swerve to avoid her. She was hurrying along the middle of the road, going his way, shoulders hunched, hands buried deep in the pockets of her light coloured mac. He fought desperately with the wheel to steady the Land Rover, braked hard and screeched to a halt in a cloud of dust.

He threw open the door and jumped out. Bella was already running across the moors, her mac trailing behind her like a cape. She was carrying a small holdall.

He chased her for perhaps fifty yards before finally catching up, but even then she didn't give in and struggled wildly like a cornered fox when he grabbed her arm.

,

"Keep fucking still or I'll hurt you," he yelled at her.

She eventually calmed down. She dropped the holdall and just stood there, her shoulders sagging, her breath coming in wheezy gasps.

Parker grabbed her arm and put his face close to hers.

"Where is he?" he said.

She looked at him. "I don't know what…"

He backhanded her, a scathing blow across the left cheek.

"Don't give me that bollocks you bitch. You're on your way to meet him now."

"No. No. I swear."

He tightened his grip on her arm.

"Now where is he?"

She spat in his face. "D'you really think I'd tell you after you tried to kill him?"

"I don't know what he's told you, but it was him who did the dirty on me."

She shook her head. "You're wrong. He was trying to help you."

"Is that so?"

"Yes it is and you know it."

"Now look," Parker said. "You've arranged to meet him somewhere haven't you?"

She shook her head again. "No. He's already gone. Ages ago."

"He's only just left the harbour in a boat. I saw him."

"That's not true."

Parker was losing patience. He said, "Where are you going?"

,

"Home."

"Liar. I've been along this road before and I know there are no houses in the direction you were heading."

"Then you didn't look hard enough," she snapped back.

"Now listen, Bella. If I have to I'll keep you here all fucking night. And you know what that'll mean. He'll have to go without you."

"Please don't," she yelled. "Just leave me alone?"

"I want you to take me to him."

"Why?" she blurted. "So you can murder him?"

"I don't want to kill him, Bella. Honest. I just want to get away from here. I give you my word. All I want is to save my own skin and the only way I can do that is to go with you on the boat."

She shrank away from him slightly. "I wish I could believe that."

"You've no option, Bella — not if you don't want to lose him."

He could tell by her expression that she was not sure what to do. He had one thing going for him, and that was her devotion to Maclean. If she wanted to leave the island with him tonight then she would have to trust him.

He said, "The sooner the both of us are away from here, the better for all concerned. There'll be no more killing."

"The jetty," she said after a moment. "I'm meeting him there."

,

TWENTY NINE

Jamie Fraser was dead when they found him - killed by two savage blows to the head. Young Rauri MacDonald was sent to deliver the news to his family who ran a small farm on the north side of the island. Rauri's father, together with Angus Campbell, picked up the body and carried it outside the tackle shed, where they laid it on the ground in front of the assembled group of islanders who had descended on the harbour after a boat was seen leaving.

They listened carefully to Greg Barrie's account of how he had been forced to drive the Land Rover and fit the engine to the boat.

When he was finished, Angus looked around at the others. He, like them, failed to make any sense of it. The boat was gone, which meant someone had taken it. But who had taken the Land Rover which had been spotted driving at speed through the village?

Angus wondered if there had been a dispute between the two villains which had resulted in them splitting up. But he also wondered if one of them had taken the boat while the other had gone for the treasure which they'd hidden somewhere. Were they planning to meet up along the coast?

"There's only one way to know what's going on," he said. "We have to find the Land Rover and go after the boat."

,

He pointed to three men at random. “You go and try to get another craft launched. There’s an outboard at Bill Cullen’s house in the village. The rest of you follow me.”

,

THIRTY

As Maclean steered the little boat into the cove, he was careful to avoid the submerged rocks. It was a manoeuvre he would not have attempted if the sea had been in a different mood. He'd seen what had happened to the cruiser and therefore had a pretty good idea what would become of the craft were it to be lobbed on to those razor sharp rocks. But his luck so far had been running in the right direction and he was feeling optimistic.

First, that blind fool Parker had failed to see him squatting on the floor behind the lobster pots—and that was despite shining the torch directly at him at one point. And then, to top it all, Parker had inadvertently prepared the way for his own hasty departure. Fortune shining down on me, he thought. About bloody time.

He could not have wished for a better night. A great calmness prevailed. The moon poured its liquid glow over the gently rolling sea and the sky was peppered with clusters of bright, twinkling stars. It wouldn't be an easy crossing to Mull. He knew that. Out there the sea might be a good deal more active and it'd be a struggle to make progress because the boat was riding low in the water under the weight of the five suitcases filled with treasure. The rest he'd had to leave behind because there was no way he could have taken them with him.

He adjusted the grip on the control and the prow went to the right. On his left there were more rocks jutting up through the water. There were bits and pieces of debris clinging to these rocks; a splinter of wood, a shredded piece of cloth — remains of the cruiser which the sea had as yet not claimed.

The engine chugged along healthily, kicking up a spray and giving him a wonderful feeling of freedom and exhilaration.

He came up against the jetty and killed the engine. The heavy silence enveloped him. He tied the rope to one of the soggy timbers, then stood in the prow, face level with the jetty boards.

"Bella," he called.

There was no sound and no sign of her. He cursed her for not being punctual.

"Bella."

Still nothing. His eyes searched the darkness.

He raised his voice slightly. "Bella. Are you there?"

He reached for the rusty ladder and pulled himself up on to the jetty, not thinking to take the rifle with him.

"Bella."

Nothing.

"Bella."

Something caught his eye up on the road. Set against the moon-flushed sky it looked for all the world like the distinctive outline of a vehicle. But Bella didn't have a car!

Suddenly, he felt naked without a weapon and he turned to go back for the rifle. But a noise to his left brought him to a halt. He spun round as two figures stepped out of the darkness.

Parker was standing behind Bella, holding her left arm with one hand whilst using the other to point the shotgun at Maclean's stomach.

"Going on a trip, Andy?" Parker said.

Parker released his grip on Bella and she strode across the distance between them and threw herself at her lover.

"Andy!" she cried. "Oh, Andy! He made me bring him to you. He said he'd keep me here if I didn't."

"Don't worry, love. It's all right."

Maclean put his arms around her and pulled her close.

"He's promised he'll not harm you, Andy. He says he just wants to leave here with us."

"Does he now." Maclean looked at Parker for a long moment, his gaze intense. "You were wrong you know," he said.

"So I've heard," Parker said.

"You should have let me explain."

Parker grinned. "You mean we should have given you time to alert your friends?"

Maclean shook his head. "That's not how it was."

"I know what I saw. It looked pretty obvious to me why you were there."

"Did it? Well, for your information I was there to try to help you."

"Really?"

Maclean ignored the sarcasm. "I was hoping I'd see you before they did. I probably could have helped you get away from there if you both hadn't jumped to a stupid conclusion."

,

"As I recall it you were quick enough to use your own gun," Parker said.

"Well, I didn't think it sensible to just stand there and let that idiot Hodge blow my brains out."

"I wasn't aiming a gun at you when you clobbered me in the shed just now."

"Don't make me laugh, Phil. You'd have done the same in my shoes. If I'd shown myself you'd have taken a shot without thinking."

Parker laughed. "So you're telling me that it wasn't on your mind that with me out of the way the treasure would be yours?"

Maclean's eyes flared in anger. He pushed Bella to one side and thrust out an accusing finger.

"Think back," he said. "Remember how it was. You didn't give me a chance. Before I'd even opened my mouth that crazy fool was taking aim. If only you'd listened. I had the rifle. You could have taken it and got clear of there."

"Why were you there, anyway?" Parker said. "You were meant to be looking for a way off the island."

"They wanted me there. I tried to steer them away from the hill but they wouldn't listen. What more could I have done?"

"You could have revealed yourself to me down at the harbour," Parker said. "But you didn't."

Maclean shrugged. "In my position you would have done the same. I couldn't risk you going for me."

Parker thought for a moment and said, "I take it the treasure's in the boat?"

,

Maclean nodded. “Some of it. There’s enough for us to split it between us. So why don’t we just climb aboard and go?”

Parker started to say something, but Maclean held up his hands and said, “Look, we haven't got all night. This clear weather may not last much longer. There's nearly ten miles of sea between here and Mull, so it's best we get going now.”

“And there's fog coming,” Bella cut in.

Maclean turned, a worried look on his face. “How'd you know?”

“I heard it on the radio before I left home. They said it's moving in now from the north.”

“That's all we need,” Maclean said. He turned to Parker. “Well, what's it to be, Phil? Do we go together and split the treasure down the middle, or do you kill us and go alone?”

Parker eased his forefinger off the trigger and lowered the shotgun.

“Okay, let’s go,” he said.

Maclean smiled “I'm glad you've seen sense.”

But just then a shot rang out and Maclean watched, horrified, as blood came gushing out of Bella’s shoulder.

*

She didn't scream. She just dropped down onto her side. The bullet had entered the back of her shoulder and come out just above her chest.

,

Maclean fell to his knees beside her as more shots rang out.

"They're up on the road," Parker shouted. "A whole bleeding bunch of 'em from the sound of it."

Whump! Whump!

One bullet hit the rock near Parker's head and the other smacked into the ground inches from Bella. Obviously they don't know Bella's here, Parker thought. They're just shooting at shadows.

Ca-rack! Ca-rack!

Someone using a rifle. More bullets hitting the ground around them.

"We've got to get to the boat," Maclean called out. "She's still breathing. Can you keep me covered?"

"Yeah. Go. now."

Parker fired up the hill. He had no target in his sights. He just aimed in the general direction of the Land Rover.

Once. Twice.

Reload.

Once. Twice.

He groped in his pocket and found only two more shells. He broke the barrel and shoved them in.

Ca-rack! Ca-rack!

This time the bullets slammed into the rock in front of him.

He aimed up the hill at the flashing light from their rifles and pulled the trigger.

Once. Twice.

At the same time, Maclean lifted Bella in his arms and carried her to the edge of the jetty. Then he heaved her up on to his shoulders and descended the ladder on to the boat.

When Parker heard the engine fire up he crawled backwards away from the rock and lowered himself down the ladder. Maclean was sitting in the prow, cradling Bella's head in his lap, so Parker took the controls.

More shots were fired from the top of the hill as they cleared the little cove and the bullets plunged into the water all around them. But in thirty seconds they were clear of the rocks and out of range.

THIRTY ONE

They were a mile out when the fog came.

It rolled in from the west like a cloud on wheels, blotting out the stars one by one. The greyness swirled thickly around them, cold, clammy, oppressive. Maclean reached inside his pocket and pulled out a small lightweight compass which he handed to Parker.

"I managed to get hold of this on the island," he explained. "Just make sure we're headed north, north-east."

"How's Bella doing?" Parker asked, taking the compass.

He'd realized soon after starting out that Bella wouldn't survive the crossing. She was losing too much blood and her breathing was becoming more and more erratic.

"Not good," Maclean said. "I can't keep her awake."

When Maclean had opened her coat to look at the wound, Parker had seen it too and it had turned his stomach. The hole, when the blood was wiped away, wasn't very big, but the bullet had punctured her chest just above the right breast and he was able to speculate on the extent of the damage inside. He was surprised, in fact, that she had lasted this long.

Maclean was obviously refusing to accept the inevitable. He stroked her forehead and dabbed at

,

her wound with his already blood-soaked hanky. Parker felt genuinely sorry for him.

He looked again at the girl and reflected on the irony of it. There had been three of them on the jetty and fate had decreed that the bullet fired by one of her own people should find her — the one among them whose only crime was that she had fallen in love with a man who was not deserving of it.

Parker stared ahead into the fog. The water was mirror-flat almost and he knew that probably meant a storm was brewing. Maclean continued to swab Bella's wound and her breathing gradually grew fainter.

Five minutes into the fog, the engine began to stutter. Maclean was too preoccupied to notice, but Parker became instantly aware of the change in the engine note.

His first thought was that they were running out of petrol and he prayed that this wasn't so. The islander had told him it was always kept full. But he had obviously lied.

The engine hiccoughed again.

And again.

Now Maclean was conscious of it as well and his face became so numbed by terror it seemed almost spectral against the eerie backdrop of grey, wispy cloud.

Then the engine gave a final splutter and died.

Parker reached over and unscrewed the petrol cap. Empty. Not a single bloody drop.

"You're sure it's not something else?" Maclean enquired anxiously.

,

Parker slammed his fist down on top of the outboard.

"Of course I'm sure. It's as dry as a bone."

Maclean lowered his head and stared at Bella, his expression intense. And then he broke down. The quivering of his shoulders was followed by tears that fell in large droplets on to her tangled hair.

"No. No. No," he cried.

There were no oars in the boat, so they couldn't attempt to row to Mull. They'd just have to sit tight and be carried by the current. Sooner or later, if a wave didn't swamp them, they'd be washed ashore somewhere.

For another ten minutes they drifted aimlessly without a word passing between them. Then Maclean sprang to his feet suddenly, and started yelling.

"Bella! Wake up! Bella!"

Parker watched, feeling strangely awkward, as Maclean began shaking her by the shoulders.

"Bella! Wake up! Please!"

Maclean sat astride her and started pumping her chest. Once, twice, three times. Hard enough so that if she was alive there would at least be a response. But there wasn't. Parker got up and stood over him, looking beyond his shoulders into Bella's face. Her eyes were closed and her mouth was open, but she had stopped breathing.

"She's gone, Andy," Parker said.

"No. She's sleeping. She can't be dead."

But she was. And no amount of physical stimulation was going to bring her back to life.

,

"We've got to get her to a doctor," Maclean shouted.

"A doctor won't be any use now," Parker said.

Maclean turned on Parker. "You just shut up and get that fucking engine going."

"It won't go, Andy," Parker said. "There's no petrol."

"I said get it going, dammit. We've only got a few more miles to go."

Parker could see that Maclean was on the verge of losing control of himself altogether. He backed away from him and made a move to pick up the rifle — just to be on the safe side. But Maclean suddenly pushed himself up and lunged at Parker, grabbing instinctively for the throat. Parker was knocked off balance. His knees clashed with the sharp edge of the seat and he went over, knocking his shoulder painfully against one of the rawlocks.

Maclean was on top of him at once, trying to strangle him, crying, "You killed her, you bastard. You killed her."

Parker clawed desperately at his hands but they didn't give an inch.

Maclean yelled, "If it hadn't been for you, she'd still be alive. You led them to us."

Parker placed a hand under Maclean's chin and began to push upwards.

"I'll kill you!" Maclean was yelling. "I'll kill you!"

At last his hands fell away from Parker's throat and Parker gave one final shove which sent him reeling backwards.

,

But they were both as quick as one another to get up. Maclean dived for the rifle first. But Parker had anticipated the move and was on him just as his fingers touched the barrel. They rolled to one side locked in a violent embrace, and came crashing down on the side of the boat. The deck boards reared up under their feet and the boat keeled over, throwing them both into the ice-cold water.

They both went under and Parker found himself spinning aimlessly in a vortex of flying bubbles and flailing limbs. The suitcases, weighted down with the treasure, brushed past his left shoulder towards the bottom of the sea. He rolled this way and that, did a complete somersault and swallowed mouthfuls of foul-tasting water.

Then the chaos cleared and he struggled to an upright position, trying at the same time to get his bearings. The first thing to take shape was Maclean's shrinking form. He was swimming downwards, deeper, not in some mad attempt to rescue the treasure, but trying for some absurd reason to catch up to Bella, who was sinking rapidly as water flooded her lungs.

His own insides bursting, Parker kicked out towards the surface. He broke through after a few seconds and sucked in the sweet, chilled air. The upturned boat was close by. He swam to it and clung on to dear life while he struggled to catch his breath.

Around him the sea remained calm. There was only a slight breeze to stir the fog. He felt sick, cold, helpless. The seconds ticked away and Maclean did not appear.

,

*

Twenty feet below the surface, Maclean ran out of time. Too late, he realized that he had been carried away by his emotions virtually to the point of insanity. He was holding Bella's left arm, and had been about to pull her upwards, when his lungs gave out. His nostrils flared and his eyes swelled to golf-ball size. Then his mouth fell open involuntarily and the water poured in.

He drowned in a matter of seconds.

THIRTY TWO

Parker gave up on Maclean after ten minutes. Only a fish could hold out that long under water and Maclean was no fish.

Strangely enough, he felt a deep sense of loss. Not for the treasure, which never even entered his head, but for Maclean and the islanders who had suffered and would go on suffering. The grieving widows and orphaned children. The ones who would never be able to forget the four men who had come one night to their island and had done such irretrievable damage to their lives.

The current pushed him on into the night and for over three hours his fingers, number by the cold, grasped relentlessly to the upturned hull. But eventually he lost his grip. He slid under the water, and when he came up, choking and spluttering, he was already several feet from the boat. He tried to reach it, but couldn't. He was too tired even to raise one arm to complete a single stroke. The boat continued to drift further and further away from him and in time it was swallowed by the fog.

He closed his eyes. He wanted to sleep. But at the same time he somehow found the energy to move his legs just enough to keep his body afloat. But his consciousness was slipping. Soon he wouldn't even be able to do that.

,

THIRTY THREE

"Is he dead?"

The taller of the two men knelt beside the body. It had been washed up on the beach in the early hours of the morning.

He stared for a long moment at the sand-encrusted face, the bluish colour of the skin, and the soaking wet clothes. He noticed, too, the almost imperceptible up and down movement of the man's chest.

"Aye," he said. "He's breathing. Look." The other man lowered himself to the sand and confirmed his friend's finding.

"Amazing," he said.

"What is?"

"Why, that he didn't die, of course. He must have a gut full of water though."

"I wonder how far they got."

"From the look of this one, at least a mile, I'd say."

"What could have happened? There was no storm last night as I recall. Just the fog."

"It's obvious to me. Our prayers were answered. God Himself was out there. He sent this one back so we can punish him our way."

The tall man stood up. "We should get him to Angus, then. He'll know how best to go about it."

"Aye, but let's be careful. We don't want him to die on us just yet, do we? Not until we've made the bastard suffer."

,

One took his feet, the other his arms, and they started to carry Parker along the beach towards the village.

THE END

,

,

Printed in Great Britain
by Amazon

52633778R00108